WHAt
Ever After

FAIREST OF ALL

WHATEver After

FAIREST OF ALL

SARAH MLYNOWSKI

ORCHARD

ORCHARD BOOKS

338 Euston Road, London NW1 3BH
Orchard Books Australia
Level 17/207 Kent Street, Sydney, NSW 2000

First published in 2012 in the United States by Scholastic Press,
an imprint of Scholastic Inc.

This edition published by Orchard Books in 2014

ISBN 978 1 40833 414 0

1 3 5 7 9 8 6 4 2

Printed in Great Britain
Orchard Books is a division of Hachette Children's Books,
an Hachette UK company.

www.hachette.co.uk

For Jessica Braun,

ps. Read (forever!)

* *Prologue* *

This Is Not a Joke

O nce upon a time my life was normal.

Then the mirror in our basement ate us.

Do you think I'm joking? Do you think I'm making this up? You do, don't you?

You're thinking, *Um, Abby, mirrors don't usually go ahead and slurp people up. Mirrors just hang on the wall and reflect stuff.*

Well, you're wrong. So very WRONG.

Everything I'm going to tell you is the whole truth and nothing but the truth. I'm not making anything up. And I'm not a liar, or a crazy person who thinks she's telling the truth but secretly isn't. I am, in fact, a very logical person. Fair, too. I have to be, since I'm going to be a judge when I grow up. Well, first I'm going to be a lawyer, and then I'm going to be a judge, because you have to be a lawyer first. That's the rule.

But yeah. I am an extremely logical, extremely practical, and extremely *un*-crazy ten-year-old girl whose life went completely berserk after her parents forced her to move to Smithville.

Still don't believe me? You will when you hear all the facts. You will when you hear the whole story.

Let me start at the beginning.

✳ *Chapter One* ✳

The Beginning

The moment the playtime bell rings, the kids in my new fifth-grade class decide they want to play tag. We *eenie meenie miney*, and somehow I'm it. Me, the new kid. Great.

Not.

I cover my eyes to give the other kids a ten-second head start (okay, five), then run toward the fence. Straightaway, I spot Penny, who is very tall. Well, taller than me. Although most people are taller than me. She's also wearing a bright orange jumper that's hard to miss. I don't know all the kids' names, but Penny's is easy to remember because she always wears super-high ponytails and I just think, *Penny's pony, Penny's pony, Penny's pony.*

I dash over and tap her on the elbow. 'You're it, Penny's pony! I mean, Penny.'

She looks at me strangely. 'Um, no. I'm frozen.'

Huh? It's not that cold. Plus, her orange jumper looks really warm.

'What?' I ask.

Penny wrinkles her forehead. 'You tagged me. I'm frozen.'

'Noooooo,' I say slowly. 'I was it. I tagged *you*, so now *you're* it. Now you have to tag someone else to make them be it. That's why the game is called it.' I blink. 'I mean, tag.'

'The it person has to tag *everyone*,' Penny says. Her tone suggests she knows way more about tag than I do, and my cheeks heat up. Because she doesn't. 'When you're tagged, you freeze, and the very last person tagged is the next it. It's called *freeze* tag. Got it?'

The LAST person to get tagged gets to be it? If you're the last person tagged, that means you're the best player. If you're the best player, you should get to do a happy dance while everyone throws confetti on you. You should not have to be the new it, because being it is not a reward.

My heart sinks. If I have to be it until every last fifth grader is tagged or frozen, this is going to be a very, very, VERY long game.

Here's the thing. I am trying to have a fresh start and be flexible about my new school. But how can I when the people here do EVERYTHING wrong?

Please allow me to present my case.

1. Everyone in Smithville calls Coke, Pepsi and Orange Crush soda. Ridiculous, right? *Pop* is a much better name. *Pop! Pop! Pop!* Coke *pops* on your tongue. It doesn't *soda* on your tongue.

2. The people here do not know how to make a peanut butter and banana sandwich. The right way is to slice the banana up and then press the slices one by one into the peanut butter, preferably in neat and orderly rows. But the kids in my new school mash the bananas, mix a spoonful of peanut butter into the mashed bananas, and then spread the whole gloppy mess on their bread. Why oh why would they do that?

3. And now, instead of tag, they want to play 'Ooo, Let's All Be Frozen Statues While Abby Runs Around and Around and Around.'

Ladies and gentlemen of the jury:

I do not want to call pop *soda*.

I do not want to eat gloppy banana mush.

I do not want to be it.

'I'm pretty sure the way I play is the right way,' I say, my throat tightening. I'm right. I am.

'No,' she states. 'I'm frozen. And you'd better get going, or it'll just get harder.'

Tears burn the backs of my eyes. I don't want things to get harder. I want things to be the way they used to be. Normal!

'No thanks,' I say in a careful voice that's meant not to let my tears out but might sound a little squished. Or prissy. Or spoiled-brat-y, possibly.

'You're giving up?' Penny asks. Her eyebrows fly up. 'Just because you didn't get your way?'

'No! I'm just...tired.' I'm not even lying. I *am* tired. I'm tired of everything being different. Why can't things be like they used to be?

I go to Mrs Goldman, the teacher on playground duty. I ask her if I can go to the library.

'You mean the media room, hon?' she asks.

I shrink even smaller. They don't even call a library a library here?

But the second I step into the *media room*, the world

12

gets a little better. I take a deep breath. *Ahhhh*.

Maybe in Smithville a room filled with books is called a media room, but it smells just like the library in my old, normal school. Musty. Dusty. Papery.

The books on the shelves of the school library – media room, *argh* – are books I recognise. They're books I've gobbled up many times before. Many, *many* times before.

My shoulders sag with relief, because guess what? No matter how many times you read them, stories always stay the same.

I get my love of books from my nana. She used to read to me all the time. She's a literature professor at a university in Chicago, the normal place where we used to live.

I feel a pain in my gut when I think about my old house. My faraway friends. My nana. Peanut butter and banana sandwiches made the *right* way.

And then I shake off those heavy feelings and run my finger along the row of books. My finger stops. It rests on a collection called *Fairy Tales*, where good is good, and bad is bad, and logical, practical fifth-grade girls never get stuck being it forever.

My chest loosens. Perfect.

✳ *Chapter Two* ✳

My Annoying Wake-up

That night I'm dreaming about my old friends. We're playing tag the *right* way when someone calls my name.

'Abby! Abby! Abby!'

I half open one eye. It's Jonah, my seven-year-old brother, so I pull my bedspread over my head. Sure, I love the kid, but I'm a growing girl. I need my sleep.

Jonah yanks down the covers, presses his mouth to my ear, and says, 'Abby, Abby, Abby, Abby, Abby, ABBY!'

I groan. 'Jonah! I'm asleep!'

'Wake up, wake up, wake up!'

Does he have to repeat everything a million times? There's a fine line between being persistent and being annoying.

'Go back to bed,' I order. I have been told that I can be bossy, but come on. It's the middle of the night. Plus, it's my job as an older sister to boss Jonah around. I'm only performing my sisterly duty.

It's also my job to make sure he eats his vegetables.

At dinner, I caught him hiding his broccoli in his sock. So I told on him. Then I felt guilty and gave him half my chocolate cookie.

'But the mirror is hissing,' he says now.

I squint at him. *What?* I don't even know what to do with that sentence. 'Jonah, mirrors don't hiss. They don't make any sounds at all. Unless you break them.' Uh-oh. I sit up like a jack-in-the-box. 'Did you break a mirror? That's bad luck!'

'I don't think so.' He does this weird twisty thing he sometimes does with his lips. 'Well, maybe.'

'Jonah! Which mirror?' I swing my legs over the side of my bed. It better not be my pink hand mirror, the one I once caught him using to examine his toes.

'The big one downstairs.'

'Are you kidding me? The creepy one in the basement?'

I realise I'm shrieking, and I lower my voice so I won't wake my parents. 'Why were you in the basement so late at night?' There's something odd about the mirror in our basement. It seems like it's watching me wherever I go. Like the eyes in that painting the *Mona Lisa*. But of course that makes no sense. Mirrors can't watch you. They're not alive.

He shrugs. 'I was exploring.'

I glance at my alarm clock. 'It's eleven fifty-two!' My wrist feels heavy and I realise I forgot to take my watch off before I went to sleep. I press the light. It says 11:52, too.

Jonah shrugs again.

Jonah is always exploring. It's amazing we're even related, really; we're so different. I like reading. He likes adventures. I like cuddling in my bed with a book. He'd rather be rock climbing. Seriously. Mum takes him to rock-climbing classes at the YMCA on Sundays.

Patiently, I take a breath. I ask, 'Did you see green?' because when Jonah was three, Dad got him a clock that changes colours. All night it stays red, and then at seven a.m. it turns green. Jonah is supposed to stay in bed until the clock turns green.

But Jonah isn't great at following instructions. Or colours.

'I know how to tell the time,' Jonah says, all huffy.

'Then why did you wake me up?'

'Because I saw purple, too, and I wanted to show you,' he says, then waves at me to follow him. 'Come on, come on!'

Huh? He saw purple?

I sigh. Crumbs. I get out of bed, step into my striped slippers, and follow him.

'Wait!' I say, spotting his bare feet. I steer him to his room, which is next to mine. 'You need shoes, mister. I don't want you cutting your foot on a piece of broken mirror glass.'

'But there's no glass.'

He broke a mirror and there's no glass? I point to his wardrobe. 'Shoes!' It's my job to protect all of him, even his smelly feet.

Jonah's room is bright, because of the glow-in-the-dark stars stuck to his ceiling and his *red* clock. Not purple. Red. Jonah grabs his trainers from the floor of his wardrobe and shoves them on. 'Are you happy now? Let's go, let's go!'

'Shush!' I order. Mum and Dad's door is closed, but their room is just down the hall. Mum will not be happy if we wake her up. (She already got annoyed at me once today when I told her she was six minutes and forty-five seconds late picking me up at school. I didn't mean to make her feel bad. But I have a supercool timer on my

17

watch, and if I'm not going to use it to tell her how late she is, then what am I going to use it for?)

We slink down the first flight of stairs. They creak. A lot. Finally, I reach to open the door to the basement.

I freeze. I freeze as if, well, I've been tagged. Because the truth is I am possibly not the bravest girl in the world. And it's late. And we're going to the basement.

I prefer reading about adventures to having them.

'What's wrong?' Jonah asks, sliding in front of me and down the stairs. 'Come on, come on, come on!'

I take a big, deep breath, turn on the basement light, and close the door behind me.

✳ *Chapter Three* ✳

Mirror, Mirror, Bolted to the Wall

One step. *Creak.*

Two steps. *Creak!*

Three. *Creeeeeak!*

I stop on the very bottom stair and look across the basement at the huge and creepy mirror. It's still huge and creepy, but other than that, it looks perfectly fine. 'There is not a single crack in the mirror,' I say. 'We're going back to bed. Now.'

'I never said it was *cracked*,' Jonah says. 'I said it was hissing.' He approaches the mirror, getting so close his breath turns the glass foggy. 'It must have stopped when I left.'

I stay where I am, taking in every last detail of the antique mirror the previous owners left behind. It's twice the size of me. The glass part is clear and smooth. The frame is made of stone and decorated with carvings of small fairies with wings and wands. I don't know why the old owners didn't take it with them, except... well, it's creepy. And attached to the wall. With big, heavy Frankenstein bolts.

In the reflection I see my shoulder-length curly brown hair. My lime-green pyjamas. My striped slippers. Only, there's something off about my reflection, so I turn away. I don't know *what* exactly, but it's weird.

'It's not hissing,' I say, checking out the rest of the basement. Black leather sofa. Desk. Swivel chair. Lots and lots of bookshelves, all filled with my parents' old law books, which they never look at but don't want to throw away. Mum and Dad are both lawyers. Unlike me, neither of them wants to be a judge.

For the record: I'm going to be a really great judge because I'm all about peace and order. I'll make sure justice is always served, because it's not fair when bad people don't get in trouble, or when bad things happen to good people.

Like my parents making me move to Smithville.

'You have to knock,' Jonah says.

His words pull me back. 'What's that?'

'On the mirror,' he says, his eyebrows scrunching together. 'You have to knock.'

I laugh. 'I'm not knocking on the mirror! Why would anyone knock on a mirror?'

'They would if it was an accident! See, I was playing flying crocodile when—'

'What's flying crocodile?' I ask.

'An awesome new game I invented. I'm a pirate and I'm being chased by crocodiles, except my crocodiles can fly and—'

'Never mind,' I say, regretting I asked. 'How did this lead you to the mirror?'

'Well, when I was being chased by one of the flying crocodiles—'

'One of the *imaginary* flying crocodiles.'

'— when I was being chased by one of the *imaginary* flying crocodiles, I tripped and smacked into the not-imaginary mirror. It sounded like a knock. I'll do it again. Ready?'

Ready for what? I'm ready to get back into my toasty bed. But to him I say, 'Go ahead.'

He lifts his fist and knocks.

We wait. Nothing happens.

'Nothing's happening,' I tell him.

But then I hear a low hissing sound.

Sssssssssssssssssssssss.

My whole body tenses. I do not like hissing. Especially hissing mirrors. 'Um, Jonah?'

'See? Now check this out. Look what happens when I knock twice!'

He knocks again, and a warm light radiates from the mirror, too. A warm *purple* light.

'See?' Jonah says. 'Purple! Told you!'

My mouth goes dry. What is going on? Why is the mirror in our basement turning colours? Mirrors should not change colours. I do not like mirrors that change colours!

'This is when I went to get you. But I want to see what happens if I knock again. Three's a charm, right?'

'Jonah, no!'

Too late. He's already knocking.

Our reflection in the mirror starts to shake.

I don't like shaking mirrors any more than I like purple hissing mirrors.

'What's it doing?' I whisper. My image is rippling like the surface of a lake. My insides are rippling, too. Have I mentioned that I want to be a judge because I like peace? And order? And not rippling, hissing, purple-turning mirrors?!

'It's alive!' Jonah squeals.

The ripples in the mirror spin in a circle, like a whirlpool.

'We should go,' I say as tingles creep down my spine. 'Like, *now.*' I try to pull Jonah away, but I can't. Our images are churning around and around and around in the mirror like clothes in the dryer, and we're being dragged towards the mirror. Jonah's right foot slides forward. His trainer squeaks against the concrete floor.

'It wants my foot,' Jonah cries.

'Well, it can't have it!' I grab him tight. 'You can't have it, you…you mirror-thing!' I crane my neck toward the basement stairs. 'Mum! Dad!' I yell. But they are two floors up and I closed the basement door. Why did I close the basement door? I snuck into a basement in the middle of the night and closed the door? What is wrong with me? I need backup! 'Help!'

With my free hand I reach out and grasp the leg of the desk. My fingers burn, but I will absolutely not let go of my brother *or* the desk leg.

Whoosh! Suddenly, the whole world turns sideways. Jonah and I are horizontal. We wave in the air like human flags, which makes no sense. I don't like things that make no sense.

'Cool!' Jonah hollers. Is he smiling? He is! He's

23

smiling. How could he be having fun at a time like this?

My brother's shoe disappears. Disappears right off his foot and goes into the mirror.

No! Impossible!

There's a really loud buzzing, and my brother's other shoe gets swallowed by the mirror, too.

Slurp.

My heart is racing, and I'm hot and cold at the same time, because that could not have just happened. None of this can be happening. And why weren't Jonah's shoelaces tied? Do I have to do everything myself?

My slippers are suddenly sucked off my feet.

So not my fault. You can't tie slippers.

A book flies off the bookshelf and into the mirror. And another. All my parents' law books go – *swoop* – right off the bookshelf and into the mirror, their pages flapping like the wings of overexcited birds.

The swivel chair scoots across the floor. *Slurp!*

My brother's hands are slipping. 'Abby?' he says, and for the first time tonight, my brother – who isn't afraid of anything – sounds scared.

'Hold on!' I try to tighten my grip on his hand, but our palms are clammy. Pain shoots right from my fingers to my shoulders. I ignore it. I need to hold on. I *have* to hold on.

'Abby!'

'No!' I say, holding on even tighter. He flutters in the air. His eyes are wide and glowing purple.

'Jonah!' I scream. NO, NO, NO. I will NOT let the crazy mirror slurp up my brother. I'm in charge here! I will keep my brother safe!

I let go of the leg of the desk and grab him with both hands. With a satisfied grumble, the mirror sucks us both inside.

✳ *Chapter Four* ✳

Too Many Trees

*T*hump.

I land facedown on soil. Soil and leaves and grass. There's a twig in my mouth. Blah. I pick it out and wipe my hand on my pyjama bottoms.

'I think I just broke my head,' Jonah mumbles.

'Seriously?' I ask.

'No,' Jonah says, rubbing the back of his neck. 'I'm okay.'

Good. I'm glad he's okay. Now I don't have to feel bad when I yell at him. 'WHAT WERE YOU THINKING?'

'What do you mean?' he asks innocently.

I leap to my feet and tick off the answers on my fingers.

'Exhibit A: You drag us to the basement. Exhibit B: You knock on the creepy mirror. And exhibits C, D and E: You then proceed to knock *two more times* on the creepy mirror, and when it tries to suck us in? You. Said. "COOL!"'

''Cause it was!' he exclaims. 'Come on, Abby! That was so awesome! That was the most awesomest thing to ever happen to us.'

I shake my head. I'm not sure what even happened. Where are we?

I sniff. It smells like nature. I push myself up onto my elbows and look around. I see:

1. Large trees.
2. More large trees.
3. Even MORE large trees.

Um, why are there thousands of large trees in my basement?

Wait. My basement does not have trees.

I turn to Jonah. 'We're not in the basement!'

'I know,' Jonah says, nodding. 'Sweet.'

'So where are we?'

'Somewhere awesome.'

'The garden,' I say. 'We have to be in the garden.

Right?' Except we have a tiny garden. And our garden has only two trees. Two scrawny trees. Not thousands of large trees.

'No way, we're not in the garden,' Jonah says, shaking his head.

'Maybe it looks different at night?'

'Nope. I think we're in a forest.'

'Jonah, we can't be in a forest! That's impossible!'

'Well, maybe impossible things are possible?'

He is impossible. I rub my eyes. 'This makes no sense. Wait. What if we're dreaming?'

'Both of us?' he asks, raising one eyebrow.

'Fine, me. What if I'm dreaming?'

He pinches me.

'Ow!'

'Not dreaming,' he proclaims. He bounces on his toes. 'You are one hundred percent awake, and so am I, and we are in a forest. Hey, I'm hungry. Do you have any Cheetos?'

'*Cheetos?*' I screech. 'We've somehow been transported from our basement to a forest in the middle of the night, and you're thinking about *Cheetos*?'

He scratches his belly. 'The mirror was hungry, so it ate us. Now I'm hungry, and I would really like some Flamin' Hot Cheetos. And maybe some ketchup.'

'That is disgusting,' I say. Jonah dips everything in ketchup. Even French toast.

'And it's not the middle of the night,' he continues. 'Look.'

I tilt my head. Blue sky peeks through the tops of the trees.

Before, it was night. Now it's day.

I don't understand what's going on! I stomp my foot like a two-year-old. *Ouch.* A twig scratches my heel, because – *ohhhh*, that's right – before the mirror ate me, the mirror ate my slippers. But here I am, so where are my fuzzy striped slippers?

First I will find my slippers. Then I will figure out how to get back to our basement.

That is my plan. Plans make me happy.

Step One: Find footwear.

I crane my neck and check out the scene. In addition to me and my brother, our basement chair is lying on its side a few feet from us. Some of the books from the bookshelf are also in the grass. And there are my slippers!

'Yay!' I cheer. I run toward them and slip them on. Ah. Fuzzy striped slippers can make a person feel much better.

I turn to Jonah. 'Did you find your trainers?'

'Yup,' he says, pointing at them.

'Well, put them on, and tie the laces this time.' I wait. 'Are they tied?' I know he knows how to tie them, because I taught him. And I taught him the right way, not the baby way with two bows.

He groans and laces them extra tight.

Good. We've completed Step One. Now for Step Two: Get back to our basement. *Hmm.* That one's tougher, but nothing I can't handle.

I suppose it would help if I could figure out where we are.

We can't be very far from home, since the whole trip only took, like, a minute. There must have been a tornado, or maybe even an earthquake. Yes, an earthquake! An earthquake that tossed us a few streets away from our house! Yes! We must have hit our heads and fallen asleep and that's why it's already daytime!

Now I just have to find our way home. Time to focus.

Growl.

What was that? Nothing. I must have imagined it.

Crack.

'Did you hear that?' Jonah whispers.

'Um. No?'

Growwwl.

My heart thumps. 'Any chance it's your stomach grumbling because you're hungry?'

He scoots closer. 'Maybe it's an animal's stomach. Because the animal is hungry.'

Growwwl, crack.

'Hungry for humans,' Jonah says, sounding a bit too excited for my liking.

Crack, growwwl.

Argh! How am I supposed to focus on Step Two of my plan with scary animal-stomach noises all around me?

'I think we should go,' I tell him.

'Go where?'

Growl, crack, growl, crack, growl, crack, crack!

'Somewhere that isn't here!'

I grab his hand and we run.

✳ *Chapter Five* ✳

Hide and Seek

I never knew I could move so fast.

If I was back at school playing tag – the right *or* the wrong tag – no one would ever catch me.

That's the good news about my mad dash with Jonah. The bad news is that I have no idea which way is home, or where in Smithville we are.

I also don't know what's chasing us. But guess what? Our fast-running feet may have outrun it, because I no longer hear anything behind us. Then again, that may be because my loud huffing and puffing is drowning out all other sounds.

A sharp pain stabs my side, and I stop.

'Need...water!' Jonah pants. 'Need...food! Forget

Cheetos. I'll eat anything! But no broccoli, please!'

I lean over and try to catch my breath. 'I don't know about you, but I have yet to spot a restaurant around here. Just trees, trees and more trees.'

'Look,' Jonah says, dropping his voice. He points at something up ahead.

I look, and my heart leaps when I see that it's a person! A female adult person!

'Oh, yay!' I call, charging toward her. 'Hi, there!'

She keeps going, slipping between the trees. Did she not hear?

'Excuse me!' I cry. 'Wait! Hold on!'

Finally, she turns around. She's old – like grandparent old, but without the hot pink lipstick my nana wears – and she's wearing a black coat and holding a basket.

I wave and smile.

She glares. And continues walking.

How rude. Grown-ups aren't supposed to be rude. My nana would never be rude.

Now what am I supposed to do?

'Excuse us!' Jonah yells. 'Excuse us, excuse us, excuse us, excuse us, excuse us, EXCUSE US!'

The lady stops in her tracks and turns around again. 'What?' she barks.

Yay, Jonah! I guess being persistent can pay off.

'Do you know where we are?' Jonah asks.

'We're kind of lost,' I add. 'We were in our basement, but then we knocked on our mirror, or rather, my silly brother knocked on the mirror, and—' Maybe it's best not to go into the details. 'Well, anyway. Can you help us, please?' I give her my most charming smile. I elbow Jonah to indicate that he should do the same.

She scowls and goes back to walking.

My nana would *never* ignore two lost kids in a forest, even if they weren't us. She would walk them home, tell them to wear a hat and bring them chicken soup.

'What should we do?' I ask Jonah.

'Follow her!'

'I don't think we should,' I say. 'She's mean. I don't think she really wants us to, either.'

'Do you have a better idea?' he asks.

I chew on my bottom lip.

Jonah takes that to mean *Okay, then! Follow the mean lady it is!* and off he goes. I hesitate, then hurry to catch up.

'Quietly,' I whisper, grabbing his arm to slow him down and stop him from stomping on every branch and twig.

Mean Lady goes around a tree. We go around the same tree, then hide. She goes straight; we go straight. She goes right; we go right. We are sneaky and follow her wherever she goes. Then, even more sneakily, we hide. And follow and hide and follow and hide.

'I hope she's not lost, too,' Jonah whispers as he ducks behind a tree.

Ten minutes later, she reaches a path. Yay! Only, I still don't know where we are. Why does Smithville have forests with paths in the middle of nowhere? This place is so weird. First soda instead of pop, and now weird forests.

We follow the old lady for another five minutes, until we arrive at a house. It's a small house. It's painted white, with flowers planted in the front garden, and it's cute and tidy and welcoming. My chest feels lighter, because Mean Lady does know where she's going. She's going *here*. And it's better to follow a mean lady who knows where she's going than no one at all, right?

I pull Jonah down behind a tree as Mean Lady walks up the charming stone footpath.

She knocks on the door. Once. Twice.

No one answers.

She knocks again.

And finally, the curtain behind one of the windows twitches.

* Chapter Six *

An Apple a Day

'Someone's home!' Jonah whispers. 'Why aren't they answering?'

'If a meanie like that was knocking on your door, would you?' I ask him. He'd better not.

'I know you're there, you silly thing,' the lady says in a teasing way. She's acting a lot friendlier to the silly thing in the house than she acted toward us.

The curtain moves and the window opens. 'It's just... well, you see... I'm not allowed to answer the door,' the person inside replies.

Someone *is* home! It's definitely a girl. She doesn't sound like a kid, but she doesn't sound like a grown-up, either. A teenager, maybe?

The old lady pulls a shiny red apple out of her basket. It glistens in the sun.

'Hungry,' Jonah whispers. He pretends to be a zombie and makes his eyes glaze over. '*Hhhhuungry!*'

I pinch him. 'Shhh!'

'I have apples to sell,' the lady singsongs.

'No, thank you,' the girl says from behind the window curtain. 'I'm not supposed to buy anything.'

'I'll give you one as a gift,' the lady offers, then clears her throat. 'I'll sell the rest later.'

'No, really, that's okay,' the girl says. 'But thank you.'

If I lean forward, I can see a corner of her face. Her hair is super dark, and her skin is super pale, except *not* in a zombie way. More like in a china-doll way. And her lips are really red. Really, really red. Like, blood-red, but again, not in a *bad* blood-red way. She's beautiful, actually. Also, she looks familiar, like I've seen her before. Has she babysat for us, maybe?

'But it's so yummy!' the lady coaxes, extending the apple. 'So juicy. So fresh. What's wrong? Are you concerned it might be—'

Jonah scrambles out into the open too quickly for me to catch him. 'I'll take it! I'll take the yummy, juicy apple!'

Oh, brother.

'Jonah!' I whisper-yell. '*Get! Back! Here!*'

He skids to a stop at the front door. 'Hi,' he says, smiling at the old lady. He holds out his open hand. 'Can I have one, please?'

The old lady snaps, 'It's not for you. Bye-bye, now.'

'But I said "please",' he whines. 'And I'm starving.'

I groan, then emerge from our hiding spot. 'You heard the lady. It's bye-bye time.' I grip his shoulder and lower my voice. 'Plus, you shouldn't eat food from a stranger, and you know it.'

'Then why can the girl inside eat it?' my brother asks.

Hmm. A red apple. A girl inside with dark hair and white skin. Something odd is happening in my head. It's a kind of brain squiggling, as if I should be figuring something out.

'She can't, either,' I said, distracted. 'And anyway, she's not going to. Didn't you hear her?'

To the girl, I call, 'Good job on staying safe!' I give her a thumbs-up, which the old lady swats away.

'Scoot,' the now extremely grumpy old lady says to me and Jonah. 'Time for you to go now.' She tries to smile at us, but it looks fake and a little scary. Then she turns back to the girl. 'Time for *you* to eat the apple, dear one.'

'Why is she being so unfair?' Jonah asks me. He reaches out, tilts the basket toward him, and peeks inside. 'If she's got a whole basket of apples, then why

38

can't she—' He breaks off. 'Hey. Wait a sec. The basket's *empty*, you big liar!'

The old lady wrenches the basket from him and yells, 'Go away!'

'But you said "apples",' Jonah insists. 'You said you were selling *applesssss*, so how come you only have the one you're holding?'

'I already sold the rest,' the lady says. 'All right? Are you satisfied?'

My spine is seriously tingling. Something weird is going on. I turn to the girl in the window. 'Do people often come to your door selling food? That never happens at our house, except for the Schwan's grocery delivery guy. And he drives a big truck, and it says "Schwan's" right there on the side. *And* he wears a uniform.'

'Girl Guides, too,' Jonah says, contributing. 'They come around and sell cookies.'

'True. And they wear uniforms, too, don't they?' I turn to the old lady. 'So what's the deal? If you're selling apples, why do you only have one piece of fruit?' I look at her black cloak. 'And is that supposed to be an apple-seller uniform? Because I've got to be honest – it's not, like, sending the right vibe.'

'Take the apple,' the old lady orders the girl. It seems like she's decided the best way to deal with me and Jonah is to pretend we don't exist. 'Enjoy it. It's free.'

'I don't think so,' the girl replies, her voice wobbly.

'Take it!' Beads of sweat glisten on the old lady's forehead. Make-up starts to smear down her face. Lots of make-up.

'Is your skin melting?' Jonah asks.

The girl gasps. 'It's you!' she cries, pointing to the old lady. 'You tried to trick me by wearing a disguise!' Her voice catches, as if she's frightened or about to cry or both. 'B-b-but it didn't work, so please, just go away!'

She slams the window and draws the curtains closed.

The lady stomps her feet. With her melting make-up, she no longer looks old. Just strange. The features of her face are all blurry, like if you spilled water on a painting. She mutters and says a bunch of words my nana would *never* use. She waves the apple at my brother. 'You want my apple so badly? You can have it! Go ahead! Eat it!'

Jonah grows pale. 'Never mind. I'm not really hungry any more.'

The melting old lady takes off her black cloak, exposing a tight black gown, and whips the cloak at Jonah.

'Hey!' I protest.

She draws herself tall, and something glints near her collarbone. It looks like a necklace with something hanging from it. I think it's a key, but I can't get a good enough look to be sure. Then she lifts her fists to the sky – one hand clenching the apple, the other clenching air – and roars, lion-style. She has really lost it.

She glowers at my brother. She slits her eyes, takes two steps toward him, and mutters, 'You will pay for this. You ruined my whole plan.'

How dare she! I wrap my arms around Jonah and yell, 'Don't you threaten my brother! We're not scared of you!'

What *plan* is she talking about, anyway? Just because I have a plan, she has to have a plan, too?

Except I don't have a plan. Not exactly.

The old lady laughs a terrifying high-pitched laugh. The kind that makes mirrors not just shake, but shatter.

The kind that would scare anyone.

She throws her basket on the ground and stomps back into the forest.

I feel my brother shivering.

'I think I want to go home now,' he whispers.

'Me too. And we will,' I say with fake confidence. If Jonah, who loves adventure, is scared, then the world has officially turned upside down. And if the world has turned upside down, then that leaves me to be the brave one, doesn't it? Which is a *very* frightening thought.

Think, Abby. The plan. What's the next step in the

plan? Wait, I know! Use the girl's phone! Yes! Call home! Get Mum and Dad to come and get us. If they can't get here by car, they can always try the mirror. I knock on the door. Once. Twice. Three times. I'm not giving up.

'Please go away,' the girl says wearily. 'I told you I'm not allowed to let anyone in.'

'Yes, but we aren't melty or scary,' I beg. 'My brother and I, we just need to use your phone.'

'My what?'

'Your phone!'

'I don't know what you're talking about!'

Jonah pokes me. 'Ask if she has a snack.'

'I promise we're not bad guys,' I say. 'We're just normal kids, and my brother is really hungry. Haven't you ever been lost before?'

There is silence.

I hold my breath.

Then, miraculously, the door creaks open, and we see the girl properly. She looks about the same age as my cousin, who's sixteen. She's more beautiful than I first thought, despite the frown creasing her pale skin.

'I'm going to get in trouble for this,' she says. She presses her red lips together and swings the door wider. 'But all right. You can come in.'

✳ *Chapter Seven* ✳

Hello, Snow

'I'm Abby, and this is my brother, Jonah,' I say as we follow her into the house. Except it isn't really a house. It's more of a, well, *cottage*, but that sounds like a word my nana would use.

Everything is small. Really small. Small table. Small chairs. Small lamp. And everything is tidy. Sofa cushions are plumped and upright. Table is perfectly set. Fork, plate, knife; fork, plate, knife – times eight. She must have a big family. Well, a *small* big family. But where is everybody?

'It's, uh, lovely to meet you.' The girl falters. She clutches the skirt of her dress, and I get the sense she's not used to having visitors. 'I'm Snow.'

Snow? What kind of name is Snow?

'What an interesting name,' I say, or think I say. Maybe I don't. My eyelids suddenly weigh a ton. I can barely hold them open. I yawn.

My brother pinches my arm.

Ouch! 'I'm not falling asleep!' I say, although I kind of am. It's late. And we walked for miles. And it's warm in here.

He waggles his eyebrows.

'*What?*' I say.

'Her name is *Snow*,' he says, and waggles his eyebrows again.

'Yes, Jonah,' I say, giving him a look. 'I heard.'

'*Snow*,' he repeats, giving me a look right back.

Whoa, my head feels cloudy – but that's no excuse for forgetting my manners. 'Right. Sorry. Nice to meet you, too, Snow. Do you think we could use your phone?'

'You keep saying that, but I don't know what you mean,' Snow says.

I sigh. Who doesn't know what a phone is? But I don't say that. That would be megarude. Maybe she's homeschooled. Or one of those kids who's never allowed to watch TV or use a mobile phone.

Jonah pinches me again. 'Abby,' he whispers. 'Snow is—'

'Stop it,' I mutter, and yawn again. Why is he being

44

so embarrassing? I can't take him anywhere.

'But—'

'Shush. No talking. Zip it.' When Mum or Dad tells him to zip it, he has to be quiet and silently count to a hundred.

'Would you like to sit down?' Snow asks, motioning to the sofa.

Yes! 'Thank you,' I say. My whole body aches. My feet are on fire. Walking in slippers was not my best move. If I'd known I'd be hiking through the forest when Jonah woke me up, I would have worn trainers. And kept the laces tied.

I collapse onto the sofa. So tired. Except it's hard to get comfy. These cushions are so small. Who fits on a sofa like this?

Jonah squeezes in beside me. And bounces.

'Do you have to use the toilet?' I ask him, struggling to keep my eyes open.

He shakes his head back and forth. Then he giggles. He *giggles*!

What is wrong with him? Does he ever get tired?

'Can I get you anything?' Snow asks.

'Do you have any Cheetos?' Jonah asks.

Snow looks at us blankly. 'I don't know what those are, either.'

45

Her parents must be health nuts, too.

'Do you two live around here?' she asks.

At last we're getting somewhere.

'Yes!' I say. 'I mean, no! I mean, can you just tell us how to get to Sheraton Street from here?' Realising how lame I must sound, I add, 'Um, that's where we live. We just moved.'

'I've never heard of Sheraton Street,' she says. 'So you're *really* two lost kids? You're *really* not wearing disguises?'

I laugh uneasily. 'Do people usually come over wearing disguises?'

'Only my stepmother.'

Jonah bounces again.

'Jonah, stop,' I say, and turn back to Snow. 'Why would your stepmum put on a disguise?'

'So I won't recognise her.'

I rub my forehead, because what she says makes no sense and makes total sense at the same time. It's like I'm being given puzzle pieces, one and then another and then another, and if I wasn't so tired, I could probably put all the pieces together and make some sort of picture.

'I'm glad you showed up,' Snow continues. 'Otherwise I probably wouldn't have realised it was my stepmother at the door, and I would have taken the apple. Who knows what would have happened then?'

'I do!' Jonah blurts out. 'You would have eaten the apple and it would have been poisoned. That's what!'

He zipped it up for about a minute. Not bad for Jonah. Wait. What did he just say? 'The apple would have been poisoned?'

'Yeah,' Jonah says. 'Snow's stepmum was trying to kill her with the poisoned apple and that's why she was wearing a disguise. So Snow would open the door. How could you not remember the story? Nana used to read it to you – to us – all the time!'

Stepmum.

Apple.

Disguise.

Poison.

I am suddenly wide-awake. 'Oh. My. Goodness!'

'Finally!' Jonah says, and throws his hands in the air.

No. Yes. Impossible. 'You're Snow White?' I say. 'You can't be!'

She blinks her round blue eyes. 'How do you know my last name?'

✳ *Chapter Eight* ✳

We're So Not in Smithville Any more

I look around the cottage at all the small furniture.

I think about the apple and the woman in disguise.

The stepmum in disguise.

'You're Snow White?' I ask again.

She nods.

'The *real* Snow White?'

'I think so. Unless there's another Snow White?'

'I think you're it,' Jonah says.

'But...' I slump back in my tiny chair, the gears of my brain turning.

Snow White exists only in a fairy tale. That means that if the Snow White here *is* the real Snow White, then we, Jonah and I, are also in a...in a... It makes no sense. You don't just fall through a mirror and land in a fairy tale.

'We're in the story,' Jonah says. 'It's magic!'

'But there's no such thing as magic,' I say. 'Not in the real world.'

'Maybe there is.'

'But…but…' I strain to come up with an argument that will convince him. I mean, me. I mean, him!

'You know how you want to be a judge when you grow up?' Jonah asks, his tone annoyingly calm.

'Why yes, I do know that. What does that have to do with anything?'

He shrugs. 'Judges look at the evidence, right?'

I'm silent.

'So look at the evidence,' he says.

I don't want to. But I do. I study the girl in front of me:

- Black hair.
- Pale skin.
- Red lips.

Just like in the story.

I look around the cottage. Tiny sofa. Tiny table. Tiny chairs. For tiny people. *Also just like in the story.*

I turn to Jonah. 'It's really her.' I turn back to Snow. 'It's really you!'

I'm staring at Snow White. The real Snow White. I'm in her living room.

No wonder she looked so familiar. I used to have a T-shirt with her face on it! And didn't I once dress up as her for Halloween? And wait – she's on my jewellery box! The one on my dresser. She's with some other fairy tale characters, but she's definitely there. And I think she's even wearing the same dress with the puffy skirt and fitted top that she has on now.

'Who else would I be?' she asks.

'You're famous!' Jonah cheers. 'We've never met anyone famous before.'

Snow blushes. 'You mean because I'm a princess?'

'Not because of that,' I say. 'We've heard your story, like, a million times.'

'Really?' she asks, looking worried. 'From who? Xavier, the huntsman? He said he wouldn't tell anyone!'

'From books,' Jonah says. 'You're even in films.'

Her forehead wrinkles. 'I don't understand. What's a film?'

'It's a story,' I say. 'With pictures. That move.'

'But I'm right here,' she says. 'So how can I be in books and films?'

A very good question. 'I don't know,' I say honestly.

We're all silent. I'm finding this all confusing, but at the same time, I can't help feeling giddy. Because OH MY GOSH, how cool is this? I'm standing next to Snow White! I'm *in* a fairy tale!

Snow sighs. 'So you know that my stepmother is trying to kill me?'

'Yeah,' Jonah says. 'Bummer.'

'She sent Xavier, her huntsman, to kill me, but he felt bad for me,' she says. 'He let me run away, but then I got lost in the forest. I walked and ran and walked some more, and finally, I came across this cottage. And I was so tired. So I fell asleep on an empty bed, and the next thing I knew, there were seven little people staring down at me.'

We hear a rustling outside and then the door flies open.

One little man. Two little men. Three.

'Speaking of whom…' Snow says.

It's really them! 'The dwarfs!' I yell, and then clamp my hand over my mouth. Am I supposed to use the word *dwarf*?

'Hello,' says the guy in the front. He's the tallest of the seven and possibly the oldest. He has a really loud voice. 'Is something wrong?'

I remove my hand. 'I didn't mean to call you a dwarf. What am I supposed to call you?'

'I'm Alan,' he booms. 'The guy with all the hair is Bob. The super-handsome guy is Jon. That's Stan with the big teeth, Tara has the braid, Enid has pink

51

hair, and Frances has the cane.'

Tara, Enid and Frances? Three of the dwarfs are women? That is not how I remember it. Maybe the story never said if they were women or men and I just guessed they were men. Oops.

And they're definitely not like the dwarfs in the Disney version. No Sleepy, Happy or Sneezy here.

'Hi!' says Jonah. 'Nice to meet you!'

'Now you know who we are,' Alan says. 'Do you want to tell us who you are?'

'And why you're in our house?' Stan asks.

'Talk!' says Frances, slitting her eyes and lifting her cane to point it at us.

My heart skips a beat. The dwarfs are kind of scary. I push Jonah behind me to protect him.

He pushes my arm out of the way. 'I'm Jonah!' he exclaims. 'And this is awesome!'

Bob pulls on his beard. 'Snow, we told you not to let anyone in the house when we're not home!' He really does have a lot of hair. Beard hair, moustache hair, head hair. And chest hair peeking out of his shirt. 'Didn't you learn anything from the last two times you answered the door?'

'I know, I know,' Snow says. 'But they're just lost kids.'

'Yes,' I say. 'We're just lost kids. Don't hurt us!'

Alan shakes his head. 'But why do you keep talking to strangers?'

'A stranger is a friend you haven't met yet,' Snow says, and then gets a sad look in her eyes. 'That's what my father used to say.'

'We're harmless,' I promise as I raise my arms to prove I'm weaponless. 'We'd never hurt anyone.'

Snow nods. 'They saved me from my stepmother. She came back. She tried to give me a poisoned apple, but they stopped her.'

'Wow,' says Enid. She runs her hand through her pink hair.

Frances puts down her cane.

Tara tugs on her braid.

Bob tugs on his beard.

Jon continues to look handsome.

Alan nods. 'I guess we owe you a thank-you.'

'Thank you,' all the dwarfs say together.

I flush with pleasure. 'No problem.'

Jonah puffs out his chest. 'Anytime.'

'How about all the time?' Frances grunts. 'Whenever we leave her alone, her stepmum does something awful. Do you know how hard it is to find someone to clean and cook? Hey, do you guys need a place to stay, too?'

'Cool!' Jonah cheers.

'She's not just a housekeeper,' Alan says, glaring at Frances. 'She's a little sister.'

Little? She's twice the size they are.

'It's kind of sad that a princess has to cook and clean,' I say, thinking about the unfairness of it all. 'I guess you have nowhere else to go.'

'I don't mind,' Snow says. 'It gives me something to focus on. Otherwise I'd spend all day thinking about...' Her voice trails off. I know she's had a hard time lately, what with her stepmum trying to kill her and all, so I don't ask for more info.

Poor Snow. I turn to my brother. 'Jonah, we can't stay. We have to go home. When Mum and Dad wake up, they're going to be worried.' Not that it wouldn't be cool to hang out in a fairy tale for a while. How many people get to hang out with the real Snow White?

'But we don't know how to get home,' Jonah says.

'We should probably head back to the forest,' I say. 'Maybe if we go back to where we started, we'll figure it out.'

Problem is, do I remember the way back? I should have left bread crumbs along the path, like Gretel. Hey, I wonder if all the fairy-tale people know each other. 'Do you know Gretel?' I ask. 'Sister of Hansel?'

'Who?' they ask.

'Never mind.' I guess a poor, unwanted girl wouldn't know a princess.

'Can you at least stay for dinner?' Snow asks.

'Yes!' Jonah says. 'I'm starving.'

'I make the decisions around here,' I say. 'I'm the older one.' My stomach growls.

I *am* kind of hungry. We *did* do a lot of walking today.

I'm the older, responsible sibling. It's my job to make sure we refuel before setting off on another journey.

Plus, outside there are growling animals.

And stepmums who want revenge.

'All right,' I say. 'We can stay.'

* Chapter Nine *

That's the Way the Story Goes

'I don't understand,' Stan says, ripping into a piece of stew with his ginormous teeth. 'How did you know that the peasant woman was the evil queen in disguise?'

'Because we know your whole story,' I say. 'We've read it. It's called *Snow White*.'

'No,' Jonah says. 'It's called *Snow White and the Seven Dwarfs*.'

Enid straightens her pink dress. 'That's us!' she squeals. 'The seven dwarfs! We're famous!'

'I think the real one, the one written by the Grimm brothers, is just called *Snow White*.' I turn to the dwarfs. 'But you guys are definitely in it.'

'Do you have any ketchup?' Jonah asks.

'Is that a type of food?' Snow asks.

'Yes,' Jonah says. 'A delicious kind of food.'

They shake their heads.

'Never heard of it,' Snow says.

'So you're a fortune-teller?' Bob asks. At least, I think the words came from Bob. I can't see his lips moving under all that hair.

'Nope,' I say. 'We're just kids, not fortune-tellers.'

'We kind of are,' my brother says around his mouthful of stew. 'Since we know what's going to happen.' I'm surprised he's liking the stew and not hiding pieces in his sock. It's kind of gross. Snow is not the world's best cook.

Frances narrows her eyes at us. 'Are you a witch? Because we don't want any more funny business, you hear?'

I shake my head. 'Nope. No witches, no funny business anywhere.' Well, some funny business, considering that we got here via mirror.

'Where do you live?' Alan booms.

'Smithville,' I say. 'Unfortunately.'

Alan shakes his head. 'I do not know of this Smithville.'

'I'm not surprised. I'm guessing it's kind of far from here,' I say. Like, a world away. 'Where are we, anyway?'

'You're at our cottage,' Bob says.

'Yeah, but where's your cottage?' I ask.

'In the kingdom of Zamel,' Alan says.

'Zamel!' Jonah cheers. 'Great name!'

Huh? 'Zamel? Where's Zamel?'

Frances rolls her eyes. 'Here.'

So how do I get us from here to Smithville?

'Can you tell us about it?' Snow asks.

'Smithville? It's in the United States of America,' I say.

'No, I mean my story,' Snow says. 'Can you tell us how it goes?'

'Yes,' the dwarfs echo. 'Tell us, tell us! We love stories!'

I look at my brother and shrug. I guess I can tell them, since it's, um, about them. But I doubt I remember the story exactly. It's the fifth story in the *Fairy Tales* book from the library. I only got through the first two today, and I haven't heard it since before we moved. 'Once upon a time—' I stop. 'A few years ago, there was a queen.' Then what? Hmm. Oh! 'And she cut her finger. And a few drops of blood landed on the...' I forget what they landed on. What was it? Oh, right! '...snow. And the queen thought the combo of the blood and the snow looked really pretty. Wait. It was the combo of the red and the white and something black, too. Jonah, do you remember where the black came from?'

58

He shakes his head. 'I don't even remember this part.'

Jonah wasn't exactly as into Nana's stories as I was. His eyes glazed over a lot. He liked to play more than he liked to listen.

'Anyway, the queen wished that she could have a baby who had skin as pale as snow, hair as black as, um, night, lips as red as blood.'

'As pale as snow,' Bob says, nodding. 'So that's how she got her name.'

'Oh,' Snow says softly, her eyes teary. 'I never knew that my mother wished for me. I never knew that's why I look the way I look.'

'She must have loved you very much,' Tara says.

'I'm sure she did,' I say, and my eyes get a little teary, too. Because what happens next is so sad. I clear my throat. 'And then the queen died.'

A tear rolls down Snow's cheek.

Aw. Poor Snow. I reach across the table and touch her hand. 'Do you want me to stop?'

She sniffs. 'No, go on. It's just hard to hear.'

I nod. 'The king remarried. And the new queen was really full of herself. Every night she would look in her magic mirror and ask who the fairest person in town was. And every night the mirror would say that the queen was.'

Snow rolls her eyes. 'She's obsessed with that mirror. You have no idea. She talks to it constantly.'

'And then one night, when the queen asked who the fairest was, the mirror answered back, "Snow White."'

Snow yelps. 'That's why she tried to kill me? Because of that stupid mirror?'

'You *are* really pretty,' Enid says. 'Maybe the mirror isn't so stupid.'

'I had no idea that's why she wanted me dead,' Snow says. 'I thought she just wanted to tear down my room and redecorate. She *loves* to redecorate.'

'Anyway, the queen got really upset,' I continue. 'She decided if she had Snow killed, then she would go back to being the most beautiful. So she asked one of her huntsmen to kill Snow.'

Everyone at the table gasps.

Bob turns to Snow. 'But you're still here!'

Snow looks down at the table. 'I begged Xavier not to kill me. I told him I would hide and never come back to the palace.'

'Why didn't you tell us?' Frances asks.

'It was just so awful,' Snow says. 'I wanted to forget about it.'

'The huntsman felt bad for you,' I say, nodding. 'But he told the queen that he had done it. And I think he gave her the lungs and liver of some animal, pretending it was you.'

Bob slams his fists on the table. 'That's awful!'

'I remember that part!' Jonah exclaims gleefully. 'Didn't she eat them?'

I grimace. Eight sets of eyes widen in horror.

Sure, *that* he remembers.

'She is pure evil,' Tara whispers, squeezing her braid.

I nod. 'And then she went back to the mirror and asked who the fairest person in town was, and the mirror still said it was Snow.'

Stan grunts right through his big teeth. 'She must have been really miffed!'

I take another bite of stew. Gross. The dwarfs must like Snow's company, because this is disgusting.

'What's the queen's real name?' Bob asks.

'Evelyn,' Snow says.

'Evil Evelyn,' I say. Makes it easier to remember.

'She's definitely evil,' Snow says, then motions me to go on.

'So Evil Evelyn decided that instead of trusting someone else to kill Snow, she would just do it herself.'

'Wait, Abby,' my brother interrupts. 'Where's the king in all this? Didn't you ever wonder about that? How could they write a whole story about a royal

61

family and leave out the king?'

I look at Snow. 'I think he's just kind of wimpy, right?'

Her eyes tear up again. 'He's not wimpy. He's dead. He was killed in battle when I was five.'

Me and my big mouth. Poor Snow! She lost her mum and her dad? 'I'm so sorry.'

'It's okay,' she says sadly. She pushes her chair back and stands up. 'Does anyone want more stew? I made a lot.'

'No thanks,' everyone says immediately.

Everyone except Jonah. 'Me, please!'

Seriously?

Snow picks up Jonah's plate. 'No one else? We're going to have lots of leftovers.'

'So what happens next?' Bob asks.

'I forget exactly,' I say, struggling to remember. 'I think your stepmum disguises herself as an old woman and tries to kill you a few times? She uses laces?'

'It's true!' Alan says. 'She tied them so tight Snow couldn't breathe. We came home and found Snow lying on the floor. We untied them just in time.'

'And then she came back with that poisonous comb,' Enid says, running her fingers through her pink hair.

'That was terrible,' Alan says. 'We came home and found Snow lying on the floor again.'

'But we removed the comb, and saved her just in time,' Alan booms.

Frances growls at Snow, stabbing her fork in the air. 'You have to stop letting strangers into the house.' Then she points her fork at me and Jonah. 'Not counting you two. Maybe. I haven't made up my mind yet. Now finish the story.'

'Right,' I say. 'So today was her third try. She was planning on giving Snow a poisonous apple to eat. In the story Snow actually eats the apple. And by the time the you all come home, it's too late!'

They all gasp again.

'Too late!' Enid shrieks.

'You mean...' Jon says, shielding his eyes. (His *sparkly* blue eyes. Jon really is handsome. He could totally be a film star. If, you know, they made films in fairy tales.)

I nod, unable to say the words.

There's a moment of silence.

'Thank goodness you arrived when you did,' Enid says. 'You saved Snow's life.'

'We should have a parade!' Bob says.

Maybe we should. We saved Snow White. We are awesome. We are heroes! Real heroes! Yay us!

'Not true,' says Jonah. 'The prince brings her back to life in the story. Right, Abby?'

63

Oh. Right. The prince.

'He does? How?' asks Tara.

'Well,' I say, 'after you guys find her on the floor again, you put her in a' – I'm about to say *coffin*, but it sounds too scary – 'box in the forest, and then the prince comes along and saves her.'

'How can he save someone who's dead?' Frances asks.

'When he carries her off, the poisoned apple pieces fall out of her mouth and she comes back to life,' I say. 'Or something like that.'

'I thought he kissed her,' Jonah says. 'And that's what brought her back to life.'

'No,' I say. 'That's not the real story. That's the Disney version.'

'Oh, right,' Jonah says. 'But it happened in Sleeping Beauty's story, right?'

'Right,' I say.

'I like the kissing better,' Enid says.

'But that's not what happened!' I say, getting annoyed. 'I mean, happens. I mean, will happen.'

'It's romantic either way,' Tara says, swooning. I catch her glancing at Jon.

'So I don't die?' Snow asks.

I take a quick sip of water. 'Actually, you do. But then you get better when the prince saves you. And then you get married and live happily ever after.'

'Everyone lives happily ever after in fairy tales,' Jonah says.

'Not everyone,' I say. 'Not the bad guys.' Fair is fair.

'Are there fairies in the story, too?' Tara asks, wide-eyed.

'No,' I say. 'Not this one.'

'Hmph,' Frances says. 'That doesn't make sense. Then why is it called a fairy tale?'

'Who cares?' Enid says, her eyes dancing. 'So is it Prince Trevor? From the kingdom of Gamel? It has to be, right? He's the only single prince around.'

Gamel and Zamel? Seriously? 'I don't remember this prince's specific name. I think he's handsome, though.'

'As handsome as Jon?' Tara asks, and then clamps her hand over her mouth.

'Not sure,' I say, stifling a smile. 'Snow, have you ever met the prince?'

'No,' Snow says.

Frances snorts. 'I once saw Prince Trevor throw a rock at a stranger.'

'He did?' I ask. 'That's not very nice.'

She shrugs. 'Well, he *was* two years old at the time. But still.'

'A toast!' Alan calls.

They all lift their glasses.

'Snow is going to marry a prince!'

'Hip, hip, hooray! Hip, hip, hooray!'

Hmm. There is one small problem with all the hipping and hooraying.

Snow didn't eat the apple.

Which means she didn't get poisoned.

And if she didn't get poisoned, then she didn't die.

And if she didn't die, the probably handsome prince didn't bring her back to life.

So she probably doesn't marry the probably handsome prince.

Which means Jonah and I probably ruined her life.

✳ *Chapter Ten* ✳

Oopsies

'Hip, hip, hooray! Hip, hip, hooray! Hip, hip—'

'Stop!' I shout. 'Snow isn't going to marry the prince!'

'But you just said she would,' Alan says, confused.

'She was going to, but then we ruined everything. I'm so sorry. When we stopped Snow from eating the apple, we changed her story.' By we I mean Jonah, but I'm not going to throw him under the bus in front of everyone. 'If she doesn't get poisoned, the prince can't bring her back to life.'

Jonah twists his bottom lip. 'I didn't think of that.'

'We're so sorry,' I say. 'Jonah, apologise to Snow.'

'Sorry,' he mumbles, beet red.

'It's okay,' Snow says, lowering her head. 'I don't need to marry a prince. I don't mind living with the dwarfs for the rest of my life.'

'No,' I say, feeling panicked. 'No, no, no. That is not the way your story goes. You cannot stay here and clean up after them for the rest of your life!' We have to fix our mistake. We have to. Stories shouldn't change. They just shouldn't! Look what happens when they do: Snow misses out on her prince! And she has to stay and clean the dwarfs' house for the rest of her life! It's just not fair. And things need to be fair. Judges make things fair, and so will I. 'And it's not fair that Evil Evelyn gets away with her evilness. In your story, she gets punished.'

'What happens to her?' Snow asks.

'I don't remember exactly,' I say, racking my brain.

'She has to put on burning-hot shoes and dance until she dies!' Jonah chimes in.

Sure, *that* he remembers.

Snow winces. 'Ouch. That's awful.'

Frances nods. 'That sounds like something Prince Trevor would make her do. It's the rock all over again.'

'He threw a rock when he was two! Jonah used to EAT rocks when he was two.' I shake my head. 'I have to fix Snow's story.'

'Don't worry about me,' Snow says. 'I'll be fine.

You two have to get home, anyway. Your parents are going to worry.'

'No, you can't leave now,' Bob says. 'It's already dark out. It's way too dangerous. You'll stay here tonight.'

'I guess you don't have a car to drive us home in?' Jonah asks.

'We have Yopopa,' Bob says. 'Our horse.'

'He's a genius,' Alan adds.

I can't help but giggle at the horse's name. And also: can a horse be a genius? People, yes. Me, maybe. A horse named Yopopa? Doubtful.

'What's a car?' Tara asks.

'It's a horseless carriage,' I say.

Frances narrows her eyes. 'Are you sure you're not a witch?'

'Yes,' I say. 'But I don't even think a car – or Yopopa – could get us home.' Who knows what will? Who knows what's even happening at home? I glance down at my watch. It says 12:15 A.M. How is that possible? It was just before midnight when we got sucked into the mirror. And we wandered around for at least a few hours. Maybe the watch stopped because the battery ran out. Or maybe the watch stopped because time has stopped at home. Well, why not? It makes as much sense as anything. When we finally get home, it will be the same time as when we left,

69

and Mum and Dad won't have missed us at all. Perfect!

I look through the window and see that it is pretty dark outside. And scary. And anyway, I can't leave without figuring out how to fix Snow's story. I just can't. It wouldn't be fair.

'Are you sure you have room for us?' I ask. I don't want to impose.

'Of course,' Alan says.

Hello, fairy-tale sleepover! 'Then we'll stay.'

'Jonah,' I whisper angrily a few hours later. 'You just kicked me in the face!'

Unfortunately, what Alan forgot to mention was that Jonah and I would have to share a bed.

My feet are hanging over the edge, and my brother's feet are way too close to my mouth. We're sleeping on opposite ends of a mini-dwarf-sized bed in Snow's room.

How am I supposed to sleep like this? And I need to sleep. I'm so very tired. I've been up for at least a zillion hours. Okay, I'm exaggerating. Actually, I don't know how long I've been up since my watch stopped. But I know I need to get some rest if I'm going to be able to come up with a plan to fix Snow's story. And then get us home.

'Sorry,' he says. He turns. And tosses. And turns. And

tosses. 'I'm not tired. Can we go exploring? I want to see crocodiles. And dragons. And pirates. And—'

'Shush,' I tell him, motioning to the bed next to ours. 'Snow's sleeping. And you should be asleep, too. And no, we can't go exploring. We have to figure out how to fix Snow's story. And then we have to figure out how to get home.'

'You don't need to fix my story,' Snow declares. 'I'm fine here.'

'You're up,' I say. 'Did we wake you?'

'I'm not a great sleeper,' Snow admits. 'Ever since...' Her voice trails off.

'Since what?' Jonah asks.

'Since my father died,' she says softly. Even in the dark, I can see the sadness on her face. 'My mum died right after I was born, so I never really knew her. My dad remarried and then he died a few years later. And Evil Evelyn never liked having me around.'

'What was it like living with Evil Evelyn?' I ask.

Snow sniffs. 'She just ignored me. The castle had a lot of staff, so someone else would help me with my meals and clothes and things. And then one day she started glaring at me. I guess that's when the mirror told her I was pretty.'

I sigh. I feel SO bad for Snow. We have to fix her

story. It's not fair! Why should Snow have to clean and cook for the dwarfs when she should have her own palace? Why should Evil Evelyn get away with her evil behaviour? And what about the prince? If we don't fix Snow's story, she'll never meet him and she'll never fall in love and live happily ever after.

'I'm sorry we interrupted Evil Evelyn yesterday,' I tell her.

'Oh, don't worry,' Snow says. 'I'm sure my stepmother will try again. She's tried three times already.'

'Why do you keep letting her in?' Jonah asks.

She looks at her hands sadly. 'I don't know. I guess I keep hoping it's not really her. That she doesn't really hate me *that* much. My dad used to say that you have to believe the best in people.'

'Of course you should believe the best in people,' I say. 'But not when they're trying to kill you. But you're right. Evil Evelyn will definitely try again. In fact, she's probably yapping it up with her mirror right now, asking who the fairest of them all is. When the mirror says it's you, she'll start plotting a new plan to kill you.' An idea explodes in my mind like a firework. 'Wait, that's great news! Yay!'

'Um, yeah,' Snow says. 'Yay.'

'Not yay that she's going to kill you. Yay that we're going to fix your story. See, she'll probably put on another

72

disguise and then come over. And this time we won't interrupt. We'll let her poison you.'

'We will?' Jonah asks uncertainly.

'Yes! That's the point, right? Snow gets poisoned, you don't barge in asking for an apple, and the story goes on as planned.'

'But how do you know she'll use poison again?' Jonah asks. 'The first time she didn't use it. She tried to lace her to death.'

True.

Snow shivers. 'And then there was the plan to eat my lungs and liver.'

'Your stepmum has some serious issues,' I agree. 'But she did use poison the last two times. So hopefully she'll try it again.'

'She *is* a fan of poison,' Snow says.

'Exactly. So as long as it's poison again, that's what we'll do. Snow will eat the poison, she'll fall down, the dwarfs will put her in the box, the prince will find her and save her, she'll come back to life—'

'And they'll live happily ever after!' Jonah says.

Whew. I feel much better now. Everything will continue as normal. It's a perfect plan. I am such a good planner. I bet you have to be a good planner to be a judge. So you can plan people's punishments and stuff.

73

'When do you think she'll come?' Snow asks.

I flip my pillow to the cool side. 'Good question. When did she come last time?'

'Today,' Snow says.

'No, before today.'

'Yesterday.'

'And the time before that?'

'The day before yesterday.'

'Perfect,' I say with a yawn. 'Then I bet she'll come tomorrow.' Excellent. We'll take care of everything tomorrow.

First, we fix Snow's story.

Second, we figure out how to get home.

✳ *Chapter Eleven* ✳

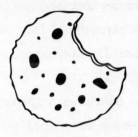

Everyone Likes Cookies

All the dwarfs are at work when I hear a knock at the door. I'm not sure what they do, but they seem very dedicated.

'That's her!' I whisper, and put down my spoon. I'm not crazy about my breakfast, anyway. Snow's porridge is no Coco Pops.

Snow turns even whiter than normal. 'Maybe I shouldn't get it.'

I place my hands on my hips. 'You have to! That's the plan.'

Jonah tugs on my arm. 'When can we go exploring?'

'Not now, Jonah,' I whisper.

'I know. But when?'

'Shush! When we're finished.'

'But I don't want to be poisoned,' Snow whines. 'I think I'd rather just live here. And stay un-poisoned.'

'I bet you won't even feel it,' I say, even though I have no idea if that's true. The story never said anything about the poison hurting, did it?

I peek behind the curtain, expecting to see the old woman from yesterday, but instead, there's a young girl standing there. She's wearing a white dress and has pigtails, and she's carrying a plate of gooey-looking cookies.

'False alarm,' I say. 'It's just a little girl.'

'Abby—' Jonah says.

'I said shush, Jonah!'

Instead of shushing, he jumps up and down. 'She changes into different disguises. It's probably Evil Evelyn dressed up.'

'Oh, right.' Duh. Of course. I should have noticed that she was still tall. It's the queen in disguise! She's so sneaky! She has poisoned cookies! 'Snow, are you ready? Let's do this! Open the door and act normal. You don't want her to suspect anything.'

'I'm sorry!' Snow yells through the curtains. 'I'm not allowed to answer the door!'

What is she doing? 'You have to answer the door! Otherwise she won't poison you!'

'You told me to act normal,' Snow says back. 'That's what I normally say.'

'Fine, but don't let her get away.'

'I have cookies!' the girl calls from outside. 'Chocolate chip cookies! I'm giving them away for free! Would you like one? I'm just a little girl! A harmless little girl!'

'This is perfect,' I whisper to Snow. 'The cookies are just like the apple. You eat the cookie, you pass out, the story goes on as normal. Case closed.' I take a step back so the little Evil Evelyn won't see me, but I pick up the corner of the curtain so I can watch. Jonah crouches behind the couch.

Snow takes a deep breath. 'Here I go!' She opens the door and looks at the little girl. 'Hello, little girl,' she says in a meek voice.

Because the door opens inward, it's blocking my view a bit. I can still see out the window, though. There's an evil glint in the girl's eyes. I can also see her freckles. Evil Evelyn went all out on this disguise. I bet she rocks at Halloween.

The queen practically shoves the plate under Snow's nose. 'Would you like one? Don't they smell delicious?'

My stomach grumbles. They *do* smell delicious. I kind of want a cookie. Especially since I didn't finish my porridge.

No poisoned cookie, no poisoned cookie!

'Well, um, all right,' Snow says, her voice shaky. 'I will eat one of your cookies.'

'Here you go,' the little girl says. 'Take your pick.'

I snort. I can't believe that Evil Evelyn thought Snow would fall for the same trick again. Obviously she's not that smart. Hmm. I almost fell for it, too.

'O-okay,' Snow says. 'Will do. I'm taking it. I'm taking it. Here I go.' She reaches outside to pick up a cookie and slowly – *verrry slowwwly* – raises it to her mouth.

No turning back now! She is going to take a bite of the cookie. The story will continue like it's supposed to. Problem solved. Now all we have to do is figure out how to get home.

Snow opens her mouth and takes a bite.

That's when I see it.

The young girl is holding a hammer behind her back.

A hammer.

A hammer?

She's lifting the hammer and swinging it toward Snow's head.

Noooooo! This is not the plan! There is no hammer in my plan!

'Stop!' I scream at the tippy-top of my lungs. I jump toward Snow and push her out of the way. We both tumble to the floor.

Snow spits the cookie out.

At the same time, the young girl's hammer swings through the air and just misses its target. 'Drat!' the young girl wails, spinning in a circle like a top.

'Why did you do that?' Snow asks me, pushing herself up on her elbows.

'She was going to hit you with a hammer!' She could have smashed Snow in half or made a dent in her head! Would a handsome prince fall in love with a smushed head? I mean, seriously. And who knows if a smushed Snow could be brought back to life?

'You again,' the young girl spits, her lips morphing into a sneer. Her make-up starts to melt and I can see Evil Evelyn beneath the disguise. And yes, she's definitely wearing a key on a chain around her neck. What, does she have to wind herself up or something?

Evil Evelyn shakes a long black fingernail in my face. Hmm. There'll be no fooling me a second time. If that key doesn't give her away, those claws sure will. 'Why are you ruining my plan?' she snarls.

Is she kidding me? 'I'm ruining your plan? You're ruining *my* plan!'

Before she can smush *me* with the hammer, I kick the door shut with my bare foot.

Evil Evelyn tries to rattle it open. 'I'm coming in! You

can't stop me!' She pushes against the door and then kicks it. Then she stops. I peek out the window. Two seconds later, she starts muttering to herself and smashing the hammer against the door.

With the next bang, the hinges almost pop off.

'Maybe this will help,' Jonah says, pushing the mini-sofa against the door.

'Good idea,' I say. 'More!' The three of us heave over the mini-dining room table and the mini-chairs. They are much lighter (and smaller) than I wish they were.

I push, Snow pushes, and my brother pushes. We will not – no, we will *not* – let Evil Evelyn in! On the other side, she's yelling and grunting and hammering. We block the door with all the furniture and appliances we can find. The rubbish bin. Chairs. A large pot. Fortunately, the windows are dwarf-sized. No way is Evil Evelyn fitting through them.

'We have to scare her away,' Jonah says.

'But how?' Snow asks.

'We have boiling water!' I scream. 'If you don't go away in three seconds, we're going to throw it at you!'

'We don't have boiling water,' Snow whispers.

'She doesn't know that,' I whisper back. I would never really throw boiling water at someone. But Evil Evelyn probably thinks all people are as evil as she is.

There's a pause.

'I'm going to throw it!' I yell, feeling a bit sick at the thought. 'You'll be covered in burns and blisters! You won't even be the second-fairest person in the land. You'll be the first ugliest!'

'I'll be back,' we hear.

Eventually the other side gets quiet.

'I think she's gone,' I say finally.

Snow looks under the curtains. 'I can't see her.' She exhales with relief.

'Now what?' Jonah asks.

Good question.

'So can we take down the blockade?' Snow asks.

I crawl over to the sofa and plant myself on a cushion. 'Let's keep it up. Just in case.'

'She only comes around once a day,' Snow says. 'We can try again tomorrow. Now help me tidy up before the dwarfs get back. Frances hates it when things are out of place.'

I feel a little queasy. 'This whole let-Snow-almost-die plan is not working. What if next time the queen comes back with a truck and mows down the cottage?'

'What's a truck?' Snow asks.

'A really big horseless carriage,' Jonah says.

'But what if she comes back with a cannon? Or a

dragon? What if she keeps coming back until she gets the job done?' I wonder aloud.

We need to save Snow's story – before there's no Snow left to save.

✳ *Chapter Twelve* ✳

Puddle Jumper

After our poisoned-cookie plan fails, I lead us back into the forest and try to retrace our steps. Not that I'm ready to go home yet. I can't leave Zamel until I figure out how to change Snow's story back to the way it was. Snow's so nice. She deserves a happy ending. It's not fair if she doesn't get one because of us. And once the story is fixed, I want to skedaddle as fast as possible. I think time has stopped in Smithville, but what if it hasn't? I don't want Mum and Dad to worry.

But first we fix the story. We HAVE to. If we don't, Evil Evelyn could return and kill Snow for real.

I can't let that happen. Snow can't DIE because of us.

I feel cold and sick just thinking about it.

'This is it,' Jonah says. 'This is where we came out.'

'How can you tell?' I ask. 'All the trees look the same to me.' Forget Yopopa. Is my brother a genius? A *nature* genius?

He points to a pile on the ground. 'I see Mum and Dad's law books. And the computer chair is behind that tree.'

Oh. Right.

'This is where you two arrived?' Snow asks. She picks up one of the law books and flips through it.

'Yup,' I say. 'Now all we have to do is figure out how to get back.'

'To get here, I knocked on the mirror three times,' Jonah says. 'What if I do that again?'

'But there's no mirror here,' Snow says.

'Good point,' Jonah says.

'What about something else with a reflection?' I ask.

Jonah points in the distance. 'Look, a puddle! Water! Water has a reflection, right?'

Yes! 'Perfect!' The three of us run toward it.

'I'm going to try,' Jonah says.

'Wait,' I say. 'But what if it works? We can't go home yet.' What if the puddle starts to pull us all toward it and then we're back in our basement? 'We still haven't fixed Snow's story.'

What if Snow gets pulled back with us? How would I explain her to my parents?

Not that they'd mind. She *is* really nice. And her cooking might be gross, but she *does* clean. She could even stay in my room. We could be BFFs. Even better than BFFs – she could be the older sister I never had but always wanted. Yes! She'd lend me her clothes, French braid my hair, and teach me how to do a handstand.

Although she wouldn't be allowed to tell Jonah what to do. That's my job. She wouldn't be allowed to tell me what to do, either.

Maybe I don't really want an older sister.

'I won't knock more than twice,' Jonah says. 'The mirror in the basement hissed when I knocked once, and then turned purple when I knocked twice. If the puddle turns purple, then I'll stop.'

'Perfect,' I say. Except I doubt this will work. There's not much of a reflection. Just a lot of mud.

Jonah drops to his knees. He lifts his hand in knocking position. He knocks. Or at least, he tries to knock. But instead, he ends up putting his fist into the dirty water.

Snow and I giggle.

Jonah looks confused. Then he says, 'Let me try again.'

He does it again. *Splash*. We giggle again.

85

'It's not hissing or turning purple,' he says, disappointment written all over his face.

I look down at the still-brown and still-silent puddle. 'Nope.'

'One more time,' Jonah says, and lifts his fist.

'Don't,' I say. 'Just in case.' What if it's too brown for us to see the purple? What if its hissing part is broken? It could still work on the third knock and drag us home!

Too late. His hand slices into the puddle. *Splash!* No purple. No hissing. Just a muddy hand.

Tee, hee. Thank goodness.

'Maybe we need to leave the way we came,' I say as Jonah wipes his hand on a leaf.

'But the cottage doesn't have a basement,' Jonah points out.

'Not a basement,' I say. 'An actual mirror.'

'Enid has a mirror,' Snow says. 'You can try hers.'

'Is it magic?' Jonah asks, his voice hopeful. 'What we really need is a magic mirror.'

Snow shakes her head. 'Sorry. I only know one person who has a magic mirror. My stepmother.'

My jaw drops. Of course! Evil Evelyn has a magic mirror! That's how Snow got into this mess in the first place. 'I bet her mirror could take us home. Or at the very least, it would know how to get us home. Since it's magic and all.'

Snow shakes her head. 'She'd never let us use it. She's not big on sharing. And we'd have to sneak in.'

'Where did Evil Evelyn get the mirror?' I ask. Maybe there are more around. Well, why not? I have one in my own basement.

'It came with the castle,' she says. 'It gets handed down from queen to queen.' Her eyes get teary. 'It used to be my mum's.'

I can feel tears in my eyes, too. Poor Snow doesn't have a mum. Or a dad.

I feel a squeeze in my stomach. I miss my mum and dad. A lot. What if I was wrong about time stopping at home? What if right now they're missing me, too?

'But I'm sure my mum never used it for evil,' Snow adds.

I blink away my tears. 'I guess we'll have to sneak in.'

Snow turns white with fear, which is no easy feat, considering she's already pretty pale. 'I'm scared. If she catches us, she'll throw us in the dungeons. Or kill us. Probably kill us.'

Jonah's eyes widen. 'Do you think she'd eat our lungs and livers, too?'

Snow nods. 'She might.'

'Do you think she'd use ketchup? I bet they'd be pretty gross without ketchup.'

I roll my eyes. 'She's not going to eat any of us, okay? We're not going to let her see us. We're *sneaking* in, not *barging* in. Anyway, maybe the mirror at the cottage will work and we won't have to even go there.'

On our way back to the cottage, Snow says, 'I have an idea about how to fix my story. But it might be silly.'

'My teacher always says there are no silly ideas,' I say. 'Only silly people. Wait, no, I don't think that's how it goes.'

Snow looks stricken. 'Do you think I'm silly?'

'Of course not!' True, she did fall for the queen's disguises multiple times. But that's because she's too nice. And anyway, I almost fell for it, too. But only once. 'You're just too trusting,' I say. 'Sometimes you let people push you around.'

She twirls her hair. 'What do you mean?'

'Well, you're a princess living in a cottage with strangers instead of your own castle. There must be some way to get back what's rightfully yours.'

She walks for a few moments without talking. 'It's just that my stepmother is so much tougher than me. I'm weak.'

'Snow, she's already tried to eat your lungs, suffocate

you, poison you, and smush you with a hammer. But you managed to survive all those attempts. You're tougher than you think.'

Snow's eyes widen. 'I didn't think of it that way.'

'Well, you should. You're one tough un-poisoned cookie. So what's your idea?'

She squares her shoulders and stands up taller. 'Well, you said that the prince finds me dead, falls in love with me, and then brings me back to life, right?'

'Exactly.'

'So why don't we just skip the dying part? I lie in the box, close my eyes and act like I was just poisoned. He comes along, falls in love, carries me home, and I spring back to life. Except I was never dead!'

I stop walking and look at her. 'So the story will basically stay the same, but you don't have to eat poison. Or have your head smushed.'

She bites her thumb. 'Silly?'

I link my arm through hers. 'Not at all. You know what? It might just work.'

A few minutes later, we're back at the cottage and knocking on Enid's mirror.

Nothing happens.

We also knock on all the shiny pots, just to be sure.

Nope. No hissing or purple anywhere.

'Now what?' Jonah asks.

'First we'll fix Snow's story,' I say. 'Then we'll have to sneak into Evil Evelyn's castle and visit the magic mirror.'

'So we get to spend another night? Yay!'

'Not yay. I'm not looking forward to another night of your feet in my face. And I don't want Mum and Dad to worry.'

'But, Abby, you said that time stopped at home,' Jonah says. 'So that means they're asleep. They don't even know we're gone!'

'I know…' I glance down at my watch. 'Wait a sec. It says one oh five A.M. My watch is working again! But really slowly. We've been here one fairy-tale day, but my watch says only an hour has passed. Hmm. Maybe time hasn't stopped at home like I thought. Maybe it's actually one oh five A.M. at home. Maybe every day here equals an hour at home.'

'So we can stay?'

'Well, Mum and Dad wake up at six forty-five and wake us up at seven. So as long as we only stay for just under six days, we'll get home before they realise we're gone.'

He shrugs. 'Easy, peasy.'

'All right,' I say. 'We'll stay. But if you kick me in the face again, I'll pull an Evil Evelyn and I'll eat—'

'My liver?' he giggles.

I snap my teeth. 'Your toes.'

* *Chapter Thirteen* *

The Hills Are Alive

The next morning, before we set off, I ask Snow if Jonah and I can borrow some clothes.

'I don't need anything,' Jonah says, looking at Snow's dress with extreme panic.

'Um, yes, you do. We've been wearing the same pyjamas for two days. We need to change.' We also need to shower, but the bathtubs here scare me. You have to bring your own water. Using the outhouse was terrifying enough.

Ten minutes later, I'm wearing a blue skirt, pink top, and a pair of sandals that belong to Snow. Snow also lent me a red ribbon that I wear in my hair like a headband. Jonah's borrowed a pair of trousers and a checkered shirt from Alan. Even though Alan's the biggest of the dwarfs, the trousers come down only to Jonah's knees, and the shirt's so tight the buttons are popping.

'I'm packing everyone stew sandwiches for lunch,' Snow calls out. 'We had so much stew left over that I made sandwiches for everyone for the rest of the week. We have tons!'

Ladies and gentlemen of the jury, what is more disgusting? Stew sandwiches or smushed-banana sandwiches. It's a close call, huh?

Jonah offers to carry the sandwiches in a leather satchel that he borrowed from Bob. It has two straps, so he's wearing it like a backpack.

The dwarfs agreed with Snow's plan and built a box for her. They have a spot they like at the top of a nearby hill, so they guess that's where they would have put the box if Snow had actually been poisoned. Unfortunately, we don't know for sure, so we have to make the best of it.

I'm not happy about making the best of it.

I would rather know exactly where we should be.

Once we carry the box up to the top of the mountain, the dwarfs wish us luck and go to work.

The plan is for Snow, Jonah and me to wait all day and then leave at night before it gets too dark. It's not like the prince is going to show up at night. I hope. Anyway, he wouldn't be able to see Snow, even in the moonlight.

Snow climbs into the box. I plump her hair and then leave the box open. He needs to see her, right?

Snow pulls out a book. It's called *Property Law 101*.

Hey! 'Is that my parents' book?'

She blushes. 'Yeah. I borrowed it from the forest. Is that okay?'

'Of course.' If she marries the prince, she might be a queen one day. And queens should have a good education.

Crack.

'An animal!' Jonah cheers. 'A dangerous animal!'

Growl.

My shoulders clench. It sounds like the animal from the other day! 'What do we do?'

Growwwl.

'It's coming from behind that tree!' Jonah exclaims, and before I can stop him, he charges toward it.

'No, Jonah!' I yell.

Growwwwwwwwwwwl.

I make a mad dash toward my brother. I will save him! I will stop the evil beast from devouring my brother! I will do whatever it takes!

The growling beast pops out from behind a tree.

It's a wild piglet.

'*Growwwwwwwwwwwl!*' the piglet cries.

'Hi,' Jonah says. 'Want to play with us?'

The pig takes one look at us and scurries away.

'Boars are easily frightened,' Snow calls out.

'Can I go and chase him?' Jonah pleads.

'No,' I snap.

'Please?'

'No.' I sit down by a nearby tree and motion for Jonah to do the same.

He stomps his feet, but does as he's told.

We wait. And wait.

'When do you think the prince will get here?'

'No idea, Jonah.'

'In five minutes? Next week?'

He's being SO annoying. 'No idea, Jonah.'

I draw a noughts and crosses board in the dirt with a stick and motion to Jonah to go first. He wins. Then I win. Then he wins.

'Let's go exploring,' Jonah says five minutes later.

'Not now, Jonah. We're waiting.'

'I'm bored of waiting,' he grumbles.

'I'm bored of you being annoying,' I grumble back. 'I'm going to check on Snow.'

Her cheeks are bright red.

'Are you okay?' I ask. 'You look hot.'

She rests the book on her stomach. 'I'm fine. Don't worry about me. Are you okay?'

95

'Snow, are you wearing sunscreen?'

Her face scrunches. 'A screen for the sun?'

'I guess you don't have ozone problems here.'

'Ozone?'

If only a modern-day dictionary had come back to fairy-tale land, too. Snow could study that.

'Let's move the box to the shade,' I say. 'We forgot water.'

'I know,' she says. 'Sorry. I should have remembered. And I'm sorry for bothering you. I'm fine.'

'Snow! It's not a bother. We don't mind. We want you to be comfortable. Come on, get out.'

Snow climbs out and stretches. There's no way it's comfy in there. The three of us heave the box a few feet to the left so it's under a tree, and she climbs back in.

'So what was it like being a princess?' I ask her.

'Oh, you know,' she says with a shrug.

'Not really. Did you go to lots of balls?'

'A few,' she says.

'Did you have a crown?'

'Yeah.'

'Lucky,' I say.

She sighs. 'You're the one who's lucky.'

'Me? I never had a crown.'

'You have a brother.'

I snort. The girl who lives in a fairy tale is calling *me* lucky? Because of my brother? My oh-so-annoying brother?

I look over at Jonah, who's building a tower with sticks. He has a very determined look on his face and his lips are doing that twisty thing.

He must feel me staring at him, because he looks up and gives me a big smile. An adorable smile.

Aw. He's a cutie.

Sure, he can be annoying, but I'm glad he's here with me. He makes Zamel – and every place, really – a little bit more fun. 'Yeah,' I admit. 'I guess I am lucky.'

She nods. 'I wish I had a brother. Or a sister.'

'I wish I had a sister, too,' I say. I look at her from the corner of my eye. 'Hey, Snow?'

'Yes?'

'Do you know how to make a French braid?'

She shakes her head.

Hmm. 'Do you know how to do a handstand?'

She nods.

'Will you show me?'

She sits up. 'And leave the box?'

'I don't think you need to stay in there the whole time. We would hear a horse coming.'

She practically jumps onto the ground. 'Let's do it,' she says.

Snow teaches my brother and me how to do handstands. Jonah learns right away. It takes me a little longer.

We're having so much fun that we barely notice when it starts to get dark.

'We should go home,' Snow says, her cheeks flushed with happiness and handstands.

So we do.

It's the next day. My watch says it's almost three A.M. in the real world. We have four real-life hours left. We have four Zamel days to get home.

We hike back up to the clearing. This time I carry a big canteen of water. Snow packs more gross stew sandwiches in Jonah's borrowed bag.

As we reach the clearing, Snow points at the box. 'Oh, look! A pillow! How nice.' She skips ahead.

'I should have brought a pillow,' I say. 'Then I could have taken a nap. I barely got any sleep last night.'

'Really?' Jonah asks innocently. 'I slept amazing.'

'You certainly took up enough room.' It wasn't just his fault I didn't sleep. I can't sleep when I'm worried. And I *am* worried. About finding a way home. About saving Snow's story. About saving Snow's life.

Wait a sec. I turn to Jonah. 'Did you bring a pillow?'

He shakes his head.

'I didn't bring a pillow,' I say. 'If you didn't bring a pillow, and I didn't bring a pillow, then who brought a pillow?'

'One of the dwarfs?'

Or…'Evil Evelyn!' we yell at the same time.

'Don't lie down!' I yell as we run towards Snow. 'Poisoned pillow, poisoned pillow!'

Snow screams. Crumbs! It's too late!

Snow pops up, the tips of her hair burnt off like she stood too close to a fire. 'Ow, ow, ow!'

I run toward her, lift the canteen, and dump it on her head.

Her hair fizzles. 'Ow, ow, ow,' she whimpers.

'Evil Evelyn is spying on us!' Jonah exclaims. 'Creepy!'

'Are you okay?' I ask, shivering.

Snow nods.

'You're still the fairest of them all,' I say.

'Sometimes I really wish I wasn't,' she says with a sigh.

✳ *Chapter Fourteen* ✳

He's Here, He's Here, He's Gone

M y stomach is a tangle of knots. We've been waiting for two days.

To help pass the time, we teach Snow how to play tag.

'Have you heard of freeze tag?' Jonah asks. 'It's so much fun. My new school friends taught it to me.'

I glare at him. 'Regular tag or nothing.'

We play regular tag. It's not that much fun with only three people. But I'm sure freeze tag would be even less fun. Then we get bored. Snow returns to reading *Property Law 101*.

'Learning anything good?' I ask.

'I am,' she says. 'I'm learning about wills.'

'What's a will?' Jonah asks.

'It's a legal document that tells people who gets a

person's possessions when she dies,' Snow says. She taps the cover. 'According to this book, a wife automatically inherits all her husband's belongings after he dies. But not if it says otherwise in his will. So I'm wondering, did my dad have a will?'

'Wouldn't you know if he did?' I ask.

'I guess,' she says with a sigh. 'It was just an idea.'

We go back to playing with sticks. Then we get bored again.

'Abby, what if the prince doesn't come today?' Jonah asks.

'He's going to come soon,' I say. He has to.

My brother fidgets with a stick. 'But what if it takes him months to come? What if it takes him years? Mum and Dad will be really cross. I don't want to miss Hanukkah. And I definitely don't want to miss my birthday. I'm getting a new scooter!'

I glance at my watch again. It's after three at home. We don't have months to wait. Even if fairy-tale months are only a couple of days in real time, we can't let my parents think we're missing. They'll call the police! They'll hang missing-kid posters around town with our pictures on them. They'll be sick with worry. I roll a twig between my fingers. 'I know we should wait for the story to unfold. I just wish we could hurry it along.'

'So why don't we just bring Snow to him?' Jonah asks. 'We'll go to his kingdom and introduce them.'

I shake my head. 'I think we should keep the story as close to the original as possible. That way we won't mess anything else up. I think it's better if he sees her in the box. The less changes from the real story, the better.'

'What if we bring the box to the palace?' Jonah asks. 'We'll put it outside his door. Then when he goes outside, he'll trip over it and the story will go back to normal.'

I snort. 'We can't carry the box all the way to Camel.'

'Gamel,' Snow says.

'Whatever.' Oh! Oh! 'I have an idea! We could send the prince an e-mail asking him to come here!'

Jonah laughs. 'An e-mail?'

I blush. 'A letter. I meant a letter. We send him a letter to say that he's wanted somewhere else, and we get him to come this way. Then he rides by and sees Snow in the box, just like in the story.'

Snow bites her lower lip. 'If he's going towards my old house, he would have to ride by here. We could tell him that he's wanted at the palace.'

'Perfect!' I squeal. 'Then he meets you along the way and the rest is destiny!'

* * *

In fairy-tale land, post is sent by postmen on horseback. We write and send a letter to the prince, telling him to come to the Zamel palace pronto, and then we wait.

And wait.

And wait.

Bor-ring.

Two days later, my watch says it's five o'clock back home. And I'm still sitting cross-legged on the forest ground, waiting.

Two more nights of Jonah's feet in my face.

Two more nights of eating Snow's gross porridge and stew.

Two more nights away from my mum and dad.

I like spending time with Snow, and I like hanging with the dwarfs at night, but I miss my parents. I miss my bed. I might even miss Smithville. I definitely miss my sofa. All this sitting in the forest is making my bum sore. I don't even want to discuss the ants trying to crawl up my legs.

I look over at my brother, who's scowling at a group of rocks. Even he's starting to get a little, well, antsy.

I know I have to try to fix Snow's story. It's the right thing to do. But we can't wait too much longer. We have to figure out how to go home.

103

B-bam, b-bam, b-bam. There's a thundering in the distance.

My heart speeds up. 'That must be him!'

'Finally!' Jonah says.

Snow sits up. '*Him*, him?'

'*Him*, him! Places, everyone!' I yell. 'Places! Go, go, go!'

Snow is supposed to run to the box. Jonah and I are supposed to climb a tree. Yes, one of the skills I've mastered while twiddling our thumbs in the forest is tree climbing. Jonah knows how since it's kind of like rock climbing, but easier. Snow wouldn't try it. She's afraid of heights. At least she's not claustrophobic. That would be bad, considering she's had to spend most of the past few days in a box.

Snow runs back to the box. I give Jonah a boost and he climbs to the top of the tree.

We hear the hooves of horses pounding in the distance.

I see a young man on a brown horse. He has blond hair, looks tall, and is really handsome. He's wearing a crown and a red cape. It must be the prince. He looks like a prince. Not that I've ever seen a prince in real life, but he looks pretty prince-y to me. 'It's him!' I cheer. 'It's really him! Our plan worked!'

He's riding right toward the box. Now he's about a

mile away! Now half a mile! He's a few yards away! He's slowing down! He's looking at the box! Any second now! Any second now, he'll see Snow and fall in love with her! The story will continue the way it's supposed to!

Wait. He's not stopping. Why isn't he stopping? He's speeding up. He's leaving. He's galloping away. Huh?

Dust flies everywhere as he gallops right past us.

I hold on to a branch, and as carefully as I can, I jump out of the tree. 'Stop!' I yell at him. 'You're supposed to stop!'

But he doesn't hear me. What, is he listening to an iPod or something? No, they definitely don't have iPods here. A Walkman, maybe?

I know it was him. It had to be. So what happened?

'That's it?' Jonah asks, sliding down to the ground. 'He's gone?'

'It can't be!' I cry. 'He saw the box. He looked right at it. Why didn't he stop?'

We hurry closer to the box. It's empty.

'Hello?' I call. 'Snow?'

No answer.

No Snow.

'Snow!' I yell louder. My heart slams against my chest. Where is she? Did Evil Evelyn do something to her? Oh, no. Poor Snow!

Squeak.

Huh? What's that? Jonah pulls on my arm and points to a tree. A white sleeve peeps out from behind the trunk.

'Snow?'

Squeak.

'Snow, why are you hiding behind the tree?'

She doesn't answer. Instead, she lets out another squeak.

'Snow, are you okay?' I approach her and put my arm around her shoulder. 'What happened?'

Her cheeks are pink. 'I hid.'

'I guessed that,' I say. 'But why?'

'I don't know!' she cries. 'I got shy.'

'You got shy? *You got shy?!*' What am I going to do with this girl? Now what? The prince – as well as the opportunity – passed us right by. And now that the prince didn't find Snow in the box, he's not going to fall in love with her. Her story is going to be totally different! What about destiny?

I glare at my brother. 'This is all your fault.'

'Me? What did I do?'

'It's your fault she didn't eat the apple!' I shout. 'And why did you have to play in the basement in the middle of the night? Why couldn't you just go to sleep like a normal kid?'

He kicks a rock with his shoe.

'And you—' I turn to Snow. 'I'm doing everything I can to help you, and you're messing everything up! Don't you want your happy ending?'

She pales. 'Maybe not. Not if it's with some meanie.'

'Throwing a rock when he was two doesn't make him a meanie!' I yell.

She crosses her arms in front of her chest. 'It doesn't make him nice.'

I stomp my foot on the ground. I am cross. So cross. Instead of going home to my family, I am sharing a bed with my brother and living in the middle of the forest so I can try to help Snow. And she doesn't even want to be helped. If she doesn't care about getting her happy ending, why should I? I shouldn't. I should just go home. It's almost morning! And what if time hasn't slowed down at home? What if my watch is just broken? Broken as in malfunctioning, not as in stopped. What if Mum and Dad have been looking for us for days? What if they're so worried they get *really* sick and have to go the hospital? 'Forget it,' I say. 'We're not helping you any more. We give up.'

Jonah's mouth drops open. 'We can't give up!'

'Yes, we can,' I snap. 'It's time to go home.' Sorry, Snow. I tried, I failed and I'm sorry.

107

'You're right,' Snow says, nodding. 'We should be focusing on getting you home. Forget about me. I don't want to marry some rock-throwing meanie anyway. Even if he is a prince. I'm fine living with the dwarfs. We should go.'

'Go where?' Jonah asks.

She takes a deep breath. 'To my stepmother's.'

✳ *Chapter Fifteen* ✳

Snow's House

We are hiding behind a tree. Waiting.

'She's off!' I say, finally, as Evil Evelyn's carriage rides away. 'How long do we have before she comes home?'

'She's usually gone for about an hour,' Snow says. 'So not long.'

Evil Evelyn is on her way to see her masseuse. Snow said she goes twice a week to get a back massage. Apparently being evil is stressful.

We ride Yopopa the horse toward the castle gate. Luckily he's a giant horse and all three of us fit on his back. I'm at the rear, Jonah is in the middle, and Snow is holding the reins. Jonah begged for front place, but there's no time for Snow to teach him how to steer and stuff. I want to go home. Now. Enough is enough!

Except...

'Maybe we should wait,' I say. 'Maybe we should try something else to fix your story.' Enough is enough, but I still feel bad for her. It's not her fault she's so shy that she blew her chance to ride off with the prince and live happily ever after.

And it's not her fault her story got messed up in the first place.

'Absolutely not,' she says. 'You need to be home with your parents. Besides, how do you know I won't get my happily-ever-after anyway? I can keep coming up with ideas on my own, you know.'

'But—' I say.

'No buts,' she says.

Wow. Is this really meek little Snow talking? She's getting tougher!

'Okay,' I say. But I still feel bad.

'Okay,' Snow says, and we trot toward the ginormous castle.

'I can't believe you grew up here,' I say with a whistle. Or a kind-of whistle. Whistling is hard.

'What do you mean?' she asks as she steers

Yopopa away from a bird.

'This place is huge!'

She shrugs. 'Well, it *is* a castle.'

And it is. A giant, beautiful castle. With guards and a drawbridge and a moat.

The drawbridge is huge. Like, twenty-five feet across and ten feet wide. And it's hanging from the castle door with big chains. I wish we had a drawbridge at home. All we have are bushes and an old screen door that creaks. Although it would make having friends over a lot more difficult.

We are trying to break into a castle. What are the chances this works?

I was worried it might be too dangerous for Snow to come with us, but she said she wanted to help. Plus, she's the one who knows her way around the castle. And anyway, the queen's not even here. As for the rest of the people in the castle, we're not exactly sure what they think happened to Snow. Do they think she's dead? Do they think she's in hiding? Who knows what Evil Evelyn's told them?

We decided to disguise Snow just in case. Enid has a pink pointy hat that we used to cover her hair, and I coated Snow's very red lips with a dusting of flour. Plus, she's wearing my lime-green pjs instead of a dress. It's not as good as the queen's disguises, but it should do.

We are ready. Snow even packed us *another* picnic of stew sandwiches. Blah. For lunch and dinner. Jonah is carrying them in the borrowed satchel again. They're kind of stinky.

We pull up to the guard standing by the bridge. Luckily the bridge is still down, since the queen just left.

'That's Arnaldo,' Snow whispers, pointing at the guard.

Arnaldo is very large. Very, very large. And he's using a sharp-looking weapon to scratch his extremely bushy black eyebrows.

'You,' he barks at us. 'Why are you here?'

My knees shake. 'We're the new decorators?' I say, except it comes out as a question.

Okay, so I lied. Not nice, I know. Lying is bad. But we need to get into the castle, and this seems like the best way. Snow said decorators were always going in and out of the palace, so we decided that if we told them that's what we are, no one would look twice.

Arnaldo glares at us. Then he glares more at Snow. He is definitely looking twice. Five times at least. 'Hmm,' he mutters.

My stomach free-falls. He recognises her.

'Hmm,' he mutters again. We are so busted.

112

'Go ahead,' the bushy-eyebrowed Arnaldo finally says. 'But leave your horse here.'

Phew! I guess my pyjamas-and-pointy-hat disguise worked. We're in!

We tie Yopopa to a tree by the bridge. Then we cross the drawbridge and approach the palace.

There's a massive round gold knocker on the door.

'I'm nervous,' Snow whispers. 'I can't believe I'm back here. And I can't believe Arnaldo didn't recognise me.'

A pretty, dark-haired maid in a grey uniform answers the door.

'It's Madeline,' Snow whispers. 'She's the maid. She knows me, too.'

'You're in disguise,' I remind her. 'Arnaldo didn't recognise you and neither will she.' I hope. I really, really hope.

'Can I help you?' Madeline asks.

'We're the decorators?' I say. Again, it sounds like a question.

'Oh,' Madeline says with a frown. 'We're not expecting you for another hour.' She gives Snow a weird look. 'Do I know you?'

'No,' Snow says, hiding behind her floppy hat. 'We've never met. Never, ever. I am not a princess. I'm a decorator.'

113

I pinch her side. Way too obvious!

But Madeline seems to buy it, because she ushers us into the foyer.

The entire room is decorated in stripes. The marble floor is in black stripes. The ceiling has purple stripes. My slippers would fit right in. No wonder Evil Evelyn wants to redecorate. I've been here four seconds and I already have a headache.

'This is the room she wants to fix up?' I ask.

'No, she just did this room last month,' Madeline says.

Seriously? 'Then where? Her bedroom?' Please be her bedroom, please be her bedroom. That would make our lives so much easier.

'The kitchen,' Madeline says.

Boo.

The kitchen is decorated all in red. Red sink, red table, red pots. I feel like I'm trapped in a giant bowl of cherry jelly.

'I'll leave you to it,' Madeline says. 'I have a lot of sewing to do. The queen's disguises don't make themselves, you know.'

We wait for her to leave before we sneak out of the kitchen. We follow Snow up two winding staircases.

'This is it,' she says at the end of a long, dark

hallway. 'Her room.' She pushes open the door and we creep inside.

Hanging on the wall is the mirror.

✳ *Chapter Sixteen* ✳

That's It?

The mirror is my size and framed in gold. If I didn't already know it could talk, I'd think it was an ordinary mirror. But then I notice a fairy carved into the bottom-right corner of the frame. Hmm. Maybe it's not so ordinary.

I hope it knows how to send us home.

Jonah runs up to it and knocks on the glass.

At first, there's no response, but then a loud voice from deep inside yells, 'Are you trying to give me a concussion?'

The voice is definitely annoyed, but I can't tell if it's female or male. Two angry blue eyes glare in the reflection. There's no nose, no lips and no chin. Just eyes.

Jonah freezes. 'Sorry,' he says in a tiny voice.

'You should be,' the mirror says. 'You have to follow the rules!'

This is my kind of mirror. I can deal with rules. I turn to Snow. 'What rules?'

'It likes when you address it twice and then ask it a question. Like, "Mirror, Mirror, how are you?"'

'I also like when you don't attack me,' the mirror grumbles.

'My brother's really sorry,' I say. 'Mirror, Mirror, can you take us home?'

'Sure,' it says. 'Now?'

'Wow,' I squeal, surprised.

'You're just going to take us home, Mirror, Mirror?' Jonah asks, sounding a little disappointed. 'No quest or anything?'

'Nope. You want to go, you can go right now, but only right now.'

'Why only right now?' I ask.

The mirror doesn't answer.

I roll my eyes. 'Mirror, Mirror, why only right now?'

'Because the queen is coming home early.'

Oh, no! 'How early, Mirror, Mirror?'

117

'Soon,' it says.

'How soon?' I ask.

The front door slams. 'I'm home!'

'She can't find us here!' Snow shrieks. 'She'll kill me and throw you in the dungeons!'

'No, she'd probably just kill you all,' the mirror says. 'The dungeons are already—'

It stops mid-sentence.

'Are already what?' I ask. 'Mirror, Mirror?'

'Pretty full,' it finishes.

I have a bad feeling about this.

'Mirror, Mirror,' I say, 'who's in the dungeon?'

'Xavier the huntsman,' it says.

Snow gasps. 'Oh, no! For sparing my life?'

'No, for spilling juice on the white carpet. Of course for sparing your life!'

'Someone woke up on the wrong side of the mirror this morning,' I grumble.

'Excuse me?!' the mirror yells.

'Nothing, nothing. Mirror, Mirror, is anyone else down there?' I ask.

'Prince Trevor,' it says.

WHAT?! Now all three of us gasp.

'That c-can't be,' I stammer.

'But it is,' the mirror says. 'He came by yesterday

118

claiming he'd been summoned by a letter. The queen thought he was attempting to overthrow her. She ordered her guards to lock him in the dungeon. Anyway,' the mirror continues, 'if you two kids want to get home, you'd better hurry up. You have about thirty seconds before she gets here.'

ARGH! This is no good. I glance down at my watch. It's just before six in Smithville. We need to go home. My parents are going to be up in less than an hour! We have to go home TODAY. But the prince is in the dungeon. Because of us. It was my idea to write him a letter. It's my fault. 'We need to save the prince,' I say solemnly.

Jonah's eyes light up. 'A quest! Let's go!'

Snow puts her hand on my arm. 'But, Abby, this could be your only chance to go home.'

I can't go home knowing someone is in a dungeon because of me. My heart thumps. 'We have to save him. And the huntsman, too. We'll get another chance to go home.'

'But—' Snow says.

'No buts,' I say.

Jonah is jumping up and down. 'We have to escape before Evil Evelyn finds us!'

I turn to the mirror. 'Is there another way out?'

The mirror clucks its tongue. 'Mirror, Mirror.'

Seriously? There's no time for *Mirror, Mirror*! 'Mirror, Mirror,' I spit out. 'Is there another way out?'

'There's the window.'

'Let's go, let's go!' I whisper, hurrying to the window. I pull back the thick purple drapes and heave open the shutters. I look outside. We're two stories high.

'Now *that's* how you break your head,' Jonah says.

I turn to Snow. 'Right now I'm kind of wishing you were Rapunzel.'

'Who?'

'Never mind. How do we do this?' I look around the room for ideas. All I see are the mirror, a wardrobe, a desk and a four-poster bed. 'Jonah, any chance you have a rope in your backpack?'

He shakes his head. 'Just stew sandwiches. Hey. I'm hungry.'

'Jonah, not now.'

He looks around the room. 'Let's use her sheet!'

'Good idea,' I say, and start stripping Evil Evelyn's bed.

'But she'll notice it's gone,' Snow says.

'She'll also notice if we're here!' I point out as I pull at the linens. 'Which is worse?'

'Good point,' Snow says, and she helps me strip the

120

bed. 'Now what?' she asks when we're done.

'She's coming, she's coming,' the mirror says, taunting us.

'You guys go first,' I say. 'I'll hold the sheet. Just slide down as far as you can and then jump.'

'What about you?' Snow asks.

'Don't worry, I have a plan. Now hurry!'

Clomp, clomp, clomp. Footsteps coming up the stairs.

We hear Evil Evelyn's voice as she trails through the hallway. 'Oh, Mirror, Mirror,' she sings. 'I have a question for yooooou…'

Snow looks like she might pass out, but I push her forward. She has to go first, because she's the heaviest, and Jonah can help me hold the sheet. Plus, I want her on the ground in case Jonah needs help. Jonah and I hold the sheet so tight that our knuckles turn white.

Snow hesitates.

'Go,' I say. 'You have to move!'

'B-b-but—'

'Go!'

With a sharp breath, she goes through the window. She slides down to the bottom of the sheet and then dangles in the air about five feet off the ground. 'Now what?' she yells.

'Now you jump!' I say.

'I can't! I'm afraid!'

'You have to! Just do it!'

She closes her eyes, which I'm not sure helps, and jumps. She lands on her bum. A startled expression crosses her face, and then she smiles.

'You're next,' I tell Jonah as I wipe the sweat from my forehead.

'But, Abby,' he says, 'who's gonna hold it for you?'

'Like I said, I have a plan. We'll do it hammock-style. You two will hold the corners and I'll jump into the sheet.'

His face squishes. 'I don't know if that's a good idea. What if you get hurt?'

Aw. He's worried about me! 'I'll be fine. Go, go! We're running out of time.'

Snow waves to him from the ground, and prickles of fear run down my spine. He's going to be okay, right? He has to be! I give him a quick hug. He climbs out the window and slides down the sheet. Then he jumps to the ground with a huge smile.

Now comes the tricky part.

Me.

Facing each other, Snow and Jonah are stretching the sheet as wide as it can go to give me room to land.

I look down. Oh, boy. Can I really do this?

I turn to the mirror. 'Mirror, Mirror, please don't tell her we were here.'

'If she asks, I have to.'

Crumbs. We stripped the bed. She's going to ask.

I hear the doorknob turn. She's here! She's coming!

I try to aim myself as best I can and —

I jump.

* Chapter Seventeen *

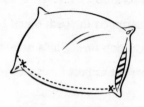

Soft Landing

I'm flying! I'm flying! I'm seriously, honestly flying!

Okay, maybe not *flying* flying, since I'm going down instead of horizontally. And whenever I imagine flying, it's usually soaring across the sky, not crashing to the ground. But still.

Yay!

Thump. I land in the sheet, and the next thing I know, I'm all tangled in it. It smells like mothballs. You'd think a fancy queen would make her stuff smell like flowers or at least fabric softener. As I remove the sheet from my head, I spot her in the window. 'You three!' she cries. 'Guards! Guards!'

I untangle myself and yell, 'Run! Run, run, run!'

Before any of the guards realise what's happening, we

make it back over the bridge. Tell me, what's the point of a drawbridge if it's never raised? I'm holding Jonah's hand to make sure I don't lose him, and Snow is right behind us. She lost her hat somewhere along the way, but I guess the disguise-ship has sailed.

Yopopa. Where is Yopopa? Yopopa is gone. 'I thought he was a genius,' I complain.

'He is,' Snow says. 'He untied himself, didn't he?'

Great.

We run into the forest. I don't look back. I honestly have never done this much running in my life.

Wzzzzz. An arrow whizzes by my head and plants itself in a tree beside me. Ahh!

Another arrow! And another!

There are arrows flying at us from all directions.

We're bending. We're dodging. We're running.

'They're going to catch us!' Jonah says, holding my hand. 'We need to hide!'

'Where?'

An arrow whizzes by. It grabs a piece of Jonah's sleeve, tears it off, and pins it to a tree trunk.

Jonah points to the top of the highest tree. 'We need to get up there.'

'But Snow can't climb,' I say.

'Time to learn,' he says. He grabs on to a

branch and heaves himself up.

'Come on, Snow,' I say to her. 'You can do it.'

I can see the fear in her eyes, but instead of saying no, she jumps for the branch. And makes it. Yay! I go next.

By the time the guards pass us, the three of us are safely hidden by a mass of branches and leaves.

We balance ourselves and catch our breath. The guards continue into the forest.

'Now what?' Snow asks.

'I'm going to have a sandwich,' Jonah says as he unties the satchel-backpack. 'I should have checked the palace for ketchup.'

'I meant, what do we DO next?' Snow asks.

I take a deep breath. 'Now we save Xavier and the prince.'

✳ *Chapter Eighteen* ✳

Castle, Take Two

We hide out in the trees and try to figure out a new plan.

Our goal is to rescue both Xavier and the prince from the dungeons.

'But the guards will be looking for us,' Snow points out. She's holding on to a large branch for dear life. 'And both dungeons are locked.'

'Of course they are,' Jonah says. He's swinging from the treetop like he's on the monkey bars. 'All dungeons are locked. Otherwise who would stay in a dungeon?'

'There's one key for both of them,' Snow says, her knuckles white.

I'm balancing on two branches. 'So where's the key?'

She shrugs.

'In Evil Evelyn's room, maybe?' Jonah says. 'If I had a key to the dungeon, I would keep it under my pillow.'

I snicker. 'It's not a baby tooth.'

'I know where you'd keep it,' he says to me. 'In your jewellery box. That's where your diary key is.'

'Jonah!' I shriek. 'Why do you know that?'

'I was exploring.' He bats his eyelashes all innocently. 'Hey Snow, did you know you're on Abby's jewellery box? Cool, huh?'

I'm definitely going to have to move that key. A memory flickers in my head. A key. I saw a key. Where did I see a key? Oh! 'Evil Evelyn was wearing a key! Around her neck!' I exclaim. In the excitement, I slip.

Snow screams, but I'm able to steady myself before I go crashing to the ground.

'Careful,' Jonah says. 'But how do we get it if it's around her neck?'

That's a very good question.

A few hours later, we head back to the castle. But this time it's the middle of the night. Luckily the moon and stars are super bright, so we can see our surroundings.

Our plan is to sneak back into Evil Evelyn's room while she's sleeping and slip off the key. The good news: the guards seem to be gone. The bad news: for the first time all day, the drawbridge is up.

'Um, how are we going to get to the castle without the bridge?' I ask.

'I guess we'll have to swim,' Snow says.

'Cool!' Jonah says.

Uh-oh. Okay, I'll admit it. I'm no Little Mermaid.

'Wait till you see my front crawl,' Jonah boasts. 'It's awesome!'

At least we won't have to swim too far. The water is only about twenty feet across. I can definitely do this. Maybe.

'What if someone sees us?' Snow asks. She pinches her nose and wades in.

Jonah runs in after her. 'How long can you hold your breath?'

I do not like where this conversation is going. 'Let's just get this over with,' I say. I take one step into the water and sink right in. Ugh, mud. And it's cold. 'Let's go, fast, fast,' I say. 'And quietly.'

Jonah is still wearing the satchel on his back. Those are going to be some very soggy sandwiches.

'Oh, no.' Snow stops her breaststroke and freezes. 'Oh,

no. Oh, no. Oh no oh no oh no. I forgot about Crowly.'

'Who's Crowly?' I ask. 'A guard?' There must be some guards roaming the area.

'No. The crocodile that lives in the moat!'

I gasp, swallowing a mouthful of water. 'This moat? Where we're swimming?' Is she kidding me?

Jonah points up ahead. 'Is that him?'

Oh. My. Goodness. Up ahead is a crocodile. A ginormous crocodile. A ginormous, scaly crocodile that's currently munching on a large bird like it's a piece of celery.

'No,' Snow says, still frozen. 'That's way too small to be Crowly. She must have had a baby.'

That's a baby? It's huge! I turn to Snow in disbelief. 'How could you forget about two crocodiles?'

'I've had other things to worry about!' she huffs. 'And when I left, there was only Crowly!'

On my left, an even bigger crocodile comes into focus. And then snaps her ginormous crocodile jaw.

'Maybe we should turn around,' I say, my voice shaking.

Baby Crocodile blocks our path from behind and snaps her baby teeth. I would probably find the idea of a baby crocodile cute if she weren't trying to eat us.

Mama Crocodile lunges again.

130

Then Baby Crocodile lunges.

Then Mama. And this time, Mama practically flies through the air.

'A flying crocodile!' Jonah hollers. 'Cool!'

Cool? Not cool! Their teeth look like steak knives!

Mama Crocodile lunges toward us. 'Shore, shore!' I yell, grabbing on to Jonah and still-frozen Snow while trying to swim on my back. I kick my legs hard. It's not easy swimming without using your arms. And Jonah is really heavy. Why is he so heavy? It's that bag he's wearing! 'What do you have in there, bricks?' I gurgle as water splashes into my mouth.

'The sandwiches!' Snow calls out. 'Give them the sandwiches!'

Jonah reaches into the satchel-backpack and pulls out three of the now soggy stew sandwiches. He tosses two at Mama. He tosses a third at Baby. Will it work?

Baby looks startled. Mama nudges one of the sandwiches with her giant mouth. She does it again. Is she sniffing it?

Suddenly, Mama chomps into it. Baby tastes hers next.

'Even crocodiles need to eat,' Jonah says, nodding.

'As long as they're not eating us,' I say.

When my feet finally touch down, Snow and I collapse on the shore in relief.

131

Not Jonah. He's giddily waving goodbye to the crocs.

Dripping wet, I stand up, my legs still shaking. 'We have to find an unlocked window on the main floor,' I say. 'I'll check these. You guys check those.'

I try three. All the shutters are sealed shut.

'They're all locked,' Snow says when we regroup.

Hmm. 'Now what?'

Snow points upward. 'Evil Evelyn's window is still open.'

'Yeah,' I say. 'But how are we supposed to get there? Fly?'

Jonah looks back at the water. 'I wonder if either of those crocs can fly...'

'Jonah, NO. This is not one of your pretend basement games. This is not flying crocodile. Crocs can't fly. And even if they could you would not be allowed to ride them. Not on my watch, anyway.' Speaking of watches... No. Mustn't look. It'll just upset me.

He shrugs and looks back at the castle. 'Oh! Some of the stones stick out just like on the rock-climbing wall at the YMCA.'

'So?' I ask.

Jonah claps his hands. 'So, we rock climb!'

What? No! 'No way,' I say.

'Yes way,' he cheers. 'It's easy. Easier than tree

132

climbing, even. I'm one of the best rock climbers in my class, you know.'

'In class you have a harness.'

'But I don't need a harness. I've never fallen.'

'You haven't fallen yet.'

'Abby,' he says, his voice serious and his lips twisty. 'I can do it. Trust me.'

'I can't do it,' Snow says, her face white. 'No more heights for me.'

'I can do it by myself,' Jonah says. 'I'll climb up. You guys spot me. I'll go in through the window. I'll take the key—'

'I am NOT letting you rock climb the outside of a castle,' I say. 'Case closed. Anyway, even if I did let you, what happens next?'

'Evil Evelyn's sleeping, right? So I carefully take off her necklace, then sneak back downstairs and open the shutters on the ground floor. You climb in and then we rescue Xavier and the prince. Then we go home.' He wipes his hands together like he's cleaning them. 'All done.'

I do not like the idea of:

1. My little brother scaling two stories of a castle wall without wearing a harness.
2. My little brother in Evil Evelyn's room by himself.

133

3. My little brother coming up with ideas when my mind is a blank. Okay, fine. I'm proud of him. But still.

'Snow, you're on spot duty,' I order. 'I'm climbing, too.'

How hard can it be?

✳ *Chapter Nineteen* ✳

It's Hard. It's Really, Really Hard.

My toes are sore. My fingers are sore. My whole body is sore. And we are only a foot off the ground.

Jonah gives me a thumbs-up. 'You're doing great!'

'Both hands on the wall!' I order. I can't believe he does this for fun.

'Don't look down!' he shouts.

So of course I do. Ahh!

We climb, and climb, and climb some more. 'Almost there,' he says. At the top he pulls himself over the windowsill and disappears inside, behind the swishy purple curtains.

'Jonah,' I whisper loudly. 'I want you to stay in view at all times!'

He pops up a second later and raises his arms in a V for *victory*. 'I did it!'

'Shhh!'

He leans over and helps me up and over the windowsill.

Right in front of us is Evil Evelyn. Luckily she's fast asleep.

'*Snooooooooooortshhhhhhhh!*'

Evil Evelyn snores. Hahahahaha. Jonah and I giggle. We can't help it.

'What's so funny?' says a voice on the wall.

My heart stops. I spin to face the mirror. How could I have forgotten about the talking mirror?

'Shhh! Please don't wake her up,' I whisper.

'Didn't hear you,' the mirror says.

'Mirror, Mirror,' I say, correcting myself. 'Shhh. Please don't wake her up.'

'That's better,' it says. Then the mirror lowers its voice. 'I won't. She's a really sound sleeper. And I don't want to get you in trouble. I like you two, and I like Snow.'

'But, Mirror, Mirror,' I say. 'If you like us so much, why did you send Evil Evelyn to kill Snow in the first place?'

'I didn't have a choice. I have to tell the queen the truth. It's part of the—'

'*Snooooooooooortshhhhhhhh!*'

136

Jonah presses his hands against the glass. 'The what? Is it a curse? Wait – are you a real person stuck in a mirror?'

'Well, I'm not in a mirror because it's a fun place to hang out.'

'That stinks,' Jonah says.

'Tell me about it. All I do is reflect, all day long. It's a constant headache.'

'What's your real name?' Jonah asks. 'Mirror, Mirror.'

'Ga-Gabrielle,' the mirror says, choking up.

Oh! She's a girl. 'Hi, Gabrielle,' I say.

'Mirror, Mirror, can I call you Gabby?' Jonah asks. 'It rhymes with Abby!'

'You may not,' the girl in the mirror says.

I'll try not to take that personally.

I tiptoe over to the queen's bed. She's sleeping on her back. Her covers are pulled up to her chin. I carefully lower them enough to see the necklace.

'*Snoooooooooootshhhhhhhh!*'

I jump. But then I lean in again. I see it! I see the key. But where's the clasp to the necklace? Oh, no! It must be at the back of her neck. How can I reach behind her head without waking her up? But wait! Someone with so many costumes would have scissors around for last-minute alterations, right? 'Gabrielle, Gabrielle,' I whisper. 'Where can I find scissors?'

137

'In the drawer of the desk,' she says.

I tiptoe to the other side of the room and open the drawer. It's a mess. There are papers, quills, bottles of ink, and – ta-da! – scissors! 'Found 'em!'

I pick up one of the papers. It says: *the fairest of all* over and over and over again.

I think back to Snow's comments earlier. I ask, 'Hey, Gabrielle, Gabrielle, do you happen to know if Snow's dad had a will?'

'Of course I know if he did,' she says. 'I know everything.'

'So did he?' I ask impatiently. 'Gabrielle, Gabrielle?'

'He did.'

No way! 'Can you tell me where it is?'

'Of course I can.'

'Look, can you please stop playing games? Just tell me! Um, Gabrielle, Gabrielle.'

'No need to get snippy, missy. It's hidden behind me. Just lift me up – carefully – and you'll see it.'

Jonah and I lift the mirror up – carefully – and gently put it down on the floor. The wall is covered with loose stones.

'You move the stones,' I tell Jonah. 'I'll get the key.'

I tiptoe back over to the queen's bed. I lean over her body…

'*Snooooooooooortshhhhhhhh!*'

I jump again. Her snores are terrifying. Must focus! Must cut the necklace!

Snap!

Done! I grab the key tightly in my fist. 'Got it. Did you find the will?'

Jonah is staring at a round hole in the wall. 'I found a bunch of papers,' he says. 'They look important.'

'Okay, put them in your bag.' I quickly help him put the stones back. 'Let's go. Gabrielle, Gabrielle, thank you for all your help. We'll be back after we've finished saving the prince and huntsman so we can go home.' Now I can't help glancing at the watch. It's after six. We're running out of time!

'Good luck!' she calls after us as we hurry out of the room.

We run down the two flights of winding stairs to the main floor. We open the shutters. Snow crawls through the small window, and we follow her to a door at the end of the hallway.

I unlock the door and peer straight ahead.

Total darkness.

'We have to go down the stairs,' Snow says.

'I can't see a foot in front of me, never mind stairs,' I say. 'Hey, Jonah, do you happen to have a

139

torch in that bag of yours?'

He scrunches his nose. 'No. But doesn't your watch have a light on it?'

'Oh! Right! Good thinking!' I press the light button on my watch and a super-scary, super-twisty creaky winding staircase pops up. 'Yikes.' This basement is SO much creepier than our basement.

'Let's go, let's go,' Jonah calls out.

'Hold the banister,' I tell him. 'And your shoelaces had better be tied.'

We wind down and down and down some more. I hold on to both the banister and the key for dear life.

When we finally reach the bottom, I take a deep breath and turn to Snow. 'Now where?'

Something runs over my foot. A rat. I clamp my hand over my mouth to avoid screaming.

In the distance, we hear rattling and then: 'Hello? Is someone there?'

'Prince Trevor?' I call out. 'Is that you?'

Jonah jumps ahead. 'We're coming, Mr Trevor. We're coming to rescue you!'

We run toward a large oval door. We all crowd our heads at the small glassless window and see the prince. He is handsome. Tall. Light hair. He looks very princely, even in this dungeon lighting. 'Hey, Snow,' I whisper, 'fix your hair, fast!' I wish it hadn't gotten frizzled by the poisoned pillow. I unlock the door and it swings open.

'Hi,' says the prince.

'Hi,' Jonah and I say back.

Snow squeaks.

'I'm Abby,' I say, and stick out my right hand to shake. But then I wonder if I should be curtsying or something, so I take my hand back. But his hand is already out, so I stick mine out again.

We shake.

'Nice to meet you,' I say.

'You too,' he says. 'Thank you for rescuing me. I'm Prince Trevor.'

'You're welcome. This is my brother, Jonah, and my very good friend Snow.'

Snow squeaks again.

I think she *likes* him. Oh! Maybe now that he sees her, he'll fall in love with her and Snow can get her happy ending after all!

And still another squeak.

'Sorry, did you say something?' the prince asks her.

She shakes her head.

Hmm. He's not going to fall in love with her if she won't even talk. Although he fell in love with her in the original story, and she definitely wasn't talking then.

141

Though her being dead probably had something to do with it. And looking pretty. Right now she's kind of a mess. She has seaweed on her forehead, and I wish she wasn't wearing my pjs. Hopefully after we finish rescuing him, they'll relax together and joke around, and they'll have a chance to talk and fall in love.

'Where's the second dungeon?' I ask Snow.

We follow her down a twisty, dark hall. She peers into another window. 'It's him! At least, I think it's him. It's so dark.'

I unlock the door and swing it open.

Inside is a guy around my dad's age. His hair is long. Really long. His beard is really long, too. He looks like Bob, but taller.

'Snow White?' he says to her. 'You're still alive?'

'Lucky for you,' I tell him. 'Let's go.'

We run back up the rickety stairs.

When we reach the main floor, I take Jonah's arm. 'We saved them. Now we go home.'

And then we hear:

Goooong! Goooong!

'What is that?' I ask, covering my ears with my hands.

Panic flashes across Snow's face. 'The alarm gong! They know we're here!'

Chapter Twenty

Run!

*G*oooong! Goooong! Goooong!

'Someone must have heard us!' Snow shrieks.

I don't care how sound a sleeper Evil Evelyn is. There's no way she's sleeping through this racket.

'We have to get out of here. Now!' Prince Trevor declares.

Plan, plan, what's the plan? 'To the moat!' I call. 'We'll swim!'

Jonah pulls my arm. 'That might not be a good idea. We're out of sandwiches.'

Crumbs. New plan, new plan! Oh! I know! 'Snow, can we lower the drawbridge?'

'Yes!' Snow says, and runs to the entranceway. 'I need help!'

Prince Trevor hurries to her side. 'What should I do?'

'Pull!' She points to the lever.

He pulls; she pulls. The twenty-five-foot bridge comes crashing down with a loud *KABLAM*.

If Evil Evelyn wasn't awake before, she is now.

'Go!' I yell, grabbing Jonah's hand. The five of us all make a run for it. Jonah and I are in the lead, Xavier is behind us, and Prince Trevor and Snow are in the back.

'Stop!' I hear.

Arnaldo and two of his fellow guards are blocking the drawbridge. They are all large. Very large. I think they even have tattoos. Snake tattoos. Or maybe they're wearing snakes. Not sure. Either way, they're scary. And their arrows are aimed at us.

We stop short. I guess there were guards roaming the grounds after all. Oops.

'Let's go back the other way,' Xavier says.

New plan! We turn around. Except Evil Evelyn has taken over the entranceway. Plus, she has a beefy guard on either side. With more snake tattoos. More arrows are pointed at us.

Now what? I look down to my right. Mama Croc has her jaw wide open and a hungry glint in her eyes. Baby Croc is on our left, looking equally hungry.

We are officially surrounded.

I am officially out of plans.

'Well, well, well,' Evil Evelyn snarls. 'Look who we have here. Guards! Put the prince and the huntsman in dungeon number one. Put the brother and sister in dungeon number two.'

Oh, no! We can't go to the dungeon! How are we going to get home if we're in the dungeon?

We're not. If we're in the dungeon, we're not going home. Never ever.

'Dungeon number two is the better dungeon,' Jonah whispers. 'I think I saw a ball.'

'That was a rat,' I tell him. 'And I don't want to be in either dungeon.'

Evil Evelyn cackles. 'As for Snow...'

'That's Snow? I thought Snow was in hiding!' one of the guards exclaims.

'I thought she was dead,' Arnaldo murmurs.

'You're both right,' Evil Evelyn says. 'She was in hiding. And soon she will be dead.'

And with that, something inside Snow appears to crack. 'NO!' she yells at the top of her lungs. 'NO, NO, NO! You are finished with trying to kill me. Do you hear me? FINISHED, FINISHED, FINISHED!' She points to the guards. 'I command you to put down your weapons!'

The queen laughs. 'You command them? You can't command them. I command them. You are nothing. You

145

clean the house of dwarfs.'

The dwarfs! Maybe they'll show up and save us! Isn't that how it always happens in the films? The heroine thinks she's about to become cat food, and then her friends swing in from the branches and save her. The dwarfs have saved Snow in the past. They're going to do it again, right?

But how will they know to save us? Hmm. Yopopa's supposedly a genius. That's probably why he rode off earlier – to get the dwarfs! And now they're going to show up in the nick of time.

Any second now.

Now.

Jonah pokes me in the ribs. 'Abby!'

'Not now, Jonah.'

'But, Abby.'

'I'm a little busy here, Jonah.' Actually, not true. But I will be, any second now. As soon as the dwarfs show up.

'Abby!' he shouts. He takes off his satchel-backpack, opens it, and shoves some papers at me. 'The will!'

The will? Oh! The will!

'We found the king's will!' I shout.

'You did?' Snow turns back to us, a look of surprise on her face.

I look at the first page, and then the second, and then the third. Please let there be something in here that helps

146

Snow. Pretty please? Pretty please with a cherry on top? Pretty please with a hundred cherries on top?

'Are you finished yet?' Evil Evelyn asks as she admires her black fingernails. 'You're boring me.'

I frantically flip through the pages. Nothing here, nothing here... Oh! Here! I found it! Page eleven, clause two! I found it! I clear my throat dramatically.

'"In case of my demise, the kingdom of Zamel will become the property of my one child, Snow White, the princess of Zamel. Queen Evelyn will remain her guardian until she is sixteen, and then Snow White will become queen."'

Everyone gasps.

'I AM sixteen!' Snow exclaims.

'I don't care if you're thirty,' Evil Evelyn snaps. 'Zamel is mine.'

'Apparently it isn't,' Arnaldo murmurs. 'You're an imposter. Snow's the queen! Get the imposter queen, boys!'

All the tattooed guards charge toward Evil Evelyn.

Yes!

'You haven't won yet!' Evil Evelyn shrieks back. 'Snow can't be queen if she's dead.'

She aims an arrow at Snow and pulls the bowstring.

'No!' I yell.

'No!' the guards yell. They jump on top of Evil Evelyn.

But it's too late. The arrow is already flying through the air.

'No!' Prince Trevor yells. In what seems like slow motion, he jumps in front of Snow.

Snow is saved! Yes!

But the arrow hits Prince Trevor square in the chest.

'Ah! Ah! Ah!' There is screaming everywhere. A lot of it is coming from me.

Prince Trevor is still standing, but his knees are shaking. After a few dramatic seconds, they buckle and he falls right over the bridge and into the water. *Splash!*

'Oh, no!' Snow cries as she jumps into the water after him. *Splash!*

'Snow!' I call out before I jump in after her. *Splash!*

'Me too!' hollers Jonah as he cannonballs into the moat.

'Jonah, NO,' I command, but – *splash!* – it's too late. Why does he never listen to me? So annoying.

Splash! Xavier jumps in, too.

Now we're all in the moat.

Unfortunately, so are the crocs.

Snap.

Snap, snap.

Snow is struggling to hold up the bleeding Prince

Trevor's shoulders while she treads water. Xavier is keeping afloat, too, while holding Prince Trevor's feet. I am holding Jonah. Mama and Baby Croc are coming toward us.

Their jaws are open.

They are growling.

They are hungry.

My mouth is dry. My heart is thumping hard against my chest.

This is it. This is really it. We will never go home again. We will never see our parents again.

I hug my shivering brother tight, close my eyes, and wait to become croc food.

✳ *Chapter Twenty-one* ✳

Still Floating

Something hits me in the face.

Croc teeth? No. It's smushy. Croc tongue?

I'm hit a second time.

'More stew sandwiches!' Jonah cheers.

My eyes pop open. Stew sandwiches are flying over the water. The crocs are happily chomping on them. Huh?

'I thought you were out of them,' I say.

'I am!' Jonah cries.

'But how…?'

Jonah points to the shore, where I see all seven dwarfs tossing sandwiches into the water.

They came! Yay! Yopopa preens himself beside them. He must have gone to get them after all. I guess he really is a genius.

While the crocs are busy stuffing their faces, we carry Prince Trevor out of the water and onto the shore.

Xavier removes the arrow. But it does no good.

Prince Trevor's eyes are closed. He's not breathing.

'Oh, no,' Jonah says. I hug him against me. I don't want him to see.

'He's gone,' I say. I can't believe it. He's really gone. And it's my fault. If we hadn't written him that letter, he wouldn't have come to the palace in the first place.

He's never going to be king.

He's never going to fall in love with Snow.

He's never going to do anything ever again.

Tears roll down my cheeks. Poor, poor Prince Trevor.

'No,' a soft voice says beside me. 'No, no, no.'

I turn around and see Snow. She's kneeling beside the prince, tears streaming down her face. 'No,' she says again, her voice hardening. 'No, no, no! You call this a happy ending? This is NOT a happy ending!'

'Snow,' I say quietly, 'there's nothing we can do.'

'But in the story, I came back to life! So why can't my prince come back to life?'

'I...I...' I have no answer. Even if I did, I feel too choked up to speak.

But then she gets a determined look on her face. She kneels down beside the prince and presses her lips

151

against his. And then it happens.

One eyelid flutters.

Then the other one flutters.

Then both his eyes fly open.

He's alive! He's alive?

'You,' Prince Trevor says, looking at Snow. 'You kissed me. I was dead, but your kiss woke me up.'

Snow nods and smiles. 'It wasn't a kiss, exactly. It was mouth-to-mouth resuscitation.'

'You know mouth-to-mouth?' Jonah asks. 'That is so cool!'

'Of course she does,' Frances says. 'With Evil Evelyn after her, we all had to learn some lifesaving measures.'

Prince Trevor sits up and beams. 'Whatever it was, you saved my life.'

'You saved my life first!' Snow says, smiling brightly. 'You jumped in front of the arrow!'

'You saved me from the dungeon first! You're amazing!'

'No, you're amazing!'

The two of them are staring dreamily into each other's eyes.

She really did save his life. And he saved hers. They saved each other.

We should have a parade!

Except this is definitely not the way the story goes. It's kind of the opposite of the way the story goes. Or at the very least, it's the story all tangled up.

Hmm. This version is different from the one in my book, but so what? Snow got a happy ending, didn't she?

Maybe sometimes different can be good?

Prince Trevor kneels on one knee. 'Snow White,' he says, 'will you marry me?'

Yay!

'Seriously?' Snow asks, raising an eyebrow. 'We just met five minutes ago.'

The girl has a point. Also, she's only sixteen. That's crazy young to get married, at least in my world.

'And I don't know you that well,' Snow continues. 'I mean, did you really used to throw rocks at people?'

'What? No!' He blushes. 'All right, maybe I did. But I was two. Can you ever forgive me?'

Snow tilts her head to the left. 'Oh, all right. I did some silly things when I was young, too. I once poured glue all over my stepmother's hairbrush.'

'She deserved it,' I say.

Speaking of Evil Evelyn, in the distance I see Xavier carrying her, kicking and screaming, into the palace. 'Let's see how you like the dungeon,' Xavier sneers.

'Listen, Trevor,' Snow says. 'I'm not looking for a

153

serious relationship right now. I need to focus on my duties here, now that I'm queen.'

'I get it,' the prince says, nodding. 'Look, why don't we take it a little slower? How about dinner?'

That's perfect! Maybe it'll take them longer to get there, but Snow and Prince Trevor will get married one day. I just know it.

Snow's eyes light up. 'I'll cook!'

'You don't have to cook anymore, Snow,' I tell her. 'You're the queen.'

'I know,' she says. 'But I like cooking.'

I hope Prince Trevor likes stew.

✳ *Chapter Twenty-two* ✳

Back to Gabrielle, Gabrielle

'This place is awesome,' Tara says, stepping into the foyer. 'You are so lucky, Snow. You have a castle and a date with a prince.' She glances wistfully at Jon.

Snow gives Tara a hug. 'I'm glad you like it, since you'll be living here with me, too.'

'We will?' Alan asks.

'Of course! I can't thank you enough for giving me a home when I needed one.'

'We're going to have to get rid of the stripes,' Frances grumbles. 'They're giving me a headache.'

Madeline the maid pops up behind them and clucks her tongue. 'More redecorating?'

'Oh, yes,' Enid says. 'We're going to need some smaller furniture. And can we paint it pink?'

I get nervous as we climb back up the staircase. The mirror is going to be able to take us home, right? 'This isn't going to be a *Wizard of Oz* situation, is it? There's not some guy hiding behind the mirror pretending to be all-powerful?'

Snow shakes her head. 'No. It's real. Where's Oz? Near Smithville?'

'Not exactly,' I say. I open the door to Evil Evelyn's room and walk straight to the mirror.

'Hi, Gabby, Gabby!' Jonah says.

'We're back. Gabrielle, Gabrielle, can we go home now?' I ask.

'You sure can,' she says.

'I'm so happy for you,' I tell Snow. 'Everything worked out. Better than I could have hoped.' I turn to the mirror. 'Can Snow set you free now that she's queen?'

'I'm afraid not,' Gabrielle says, and blinks away tears. 'But thank you for asking. I appreciate it. Now it's time to say your goodbyes.'

I'm happy and sad at the same time. I hug Alan first. 'Thanks for everything.'

Then I hug Bob and Stan.

Then Enid. 'Stay pink,' I say.

Then Jon. 'Stay handsome.'

When I hug Tara, I can't help whispering, 'Tell Jon how you feel.' She blushes.

'You're not bad, kid,' Frances says, hugging me next.

I shake the prince's hand. 'Be good to our Snow,' I say, swallowing hard to hold back tears.

'Goodbye, little man,' Prince Trevor says to Jonah.

Finally, I hug Snow. 'Will I ever see you again?' she asks.

My chest feels heavy. 'I don't know. I hope so.'

We hug tightly.

'Thank you for not letting Evil Evelyn poison me,' she says to Jonah as she ruffles his hair.

He puffs out his chest. 'No problem.'

'All right, all right!' Gabrielle grumbles. 'I have other things to do, you know.'

'Ready?' I ask Jonah.

'Ready,' he says.

I take his hand.

'The rest of you better get out of here or you might end up going, too.'

'No thanks,' Frances says. 'Horseless carriages? How does that even work?'

'Good luck,' Snow says.

I spot Tara take Jon's hand. Yay! We wave goodbye as they all leave the room.

'Hey, Gabrielle, Gabrielle, do you happen to know why the mirror in our basement brought us here in the first place?' I ask.

'You'll have to ask Maryrose,' she says.

'Who's Maryrose?' Jonah asks. 'Is Maryrose inside the mirror in our basement?'

'Maryrose will introduce herself when she's ready,' Gabrielle says simply. 'Now it's time to go.'

I sigh. I want to know more. I need to understand what happened! But right now, I really, really, really just want to go home. 'Are we going to take the furniture with us?' I ask. 'Mum would love that four-poster bed.'

'Snow would love it, too,' Gabrielle says. 'So hopefully not. But speaking of your parents, it's very important that you don't tell them anything about this.'

'But why? We tell our parents everything.' Mostly.

'It's too dangerous,' she says solemnly.

'For who?' I ask. 'Us? Them? You? Maryrose?'

'I've said too much,' Gabrielle says.

The reflection in the mirror starts to spin around and around and around. I start to see images in the swirl. A desk. Boxes. It's our basement!

'Here we go,' I say.

'What are you waiting for?' Gabrielle asks. 'I'm an open door. Come on in!'

I take a deep breath and grab Jonah's hand. Then we step through the mirror.

Zoom.

We step right onto our basement floor.

I spin around to look at the mirror. It's calm. Normal. A regular mirror.

Like nothing happened. Like nothing's weird at all.

'Hello?' I ask. 'Is anyone there?'

No one answers.

It's over. It's really over.

Well, kind of over. The basement is a mess. And all the law books are gone. So is the swivel chair. Oops.

'I wonder what happens if I knock on it again,' Jonah says, reaching out his arm.

I stop his hand mid-motion. 'Don't you dare!'

'We're home!' he cheers, running upstairs. 'Let's go tell Mum and Dad!'

'Wait,' I call behind him.

I follow my brother up the stairs. At the top of the staircase, I gently close the door behind me. The next level is awash in the morning light. I sneak into the kitchen to look at the clock on the microwave. It says 6:30 A.M. The

159

same time my watch says. So I was right after all. Time passed slower here. Unless many days have passed?

I check my mum's iPhone. According to the date, it's the morning after we left! Perfect!

'Let's go and see Mum and Dad!' Jonah exclaims.

I nod but press my finger against my lips. We creep up the last flight of stairs. I gently open their door.

'I want to get into bed with them,' Jonah whispers.

'Me too,' I whisper back. 'But we're smelly and wearing other people's clothes.' And sandals. Oops, I left my slippers at Snow's. Goodbye, slippers. I will miss you.

Jonah looks down at his too-tight outfit. 'Oh, right.'

'And I think getting into bed with Mum and Dad might freak them out.' I close their door and head towards my room.

'Good night,' Jonah says, following behind.

'Good morning,' I say back, and give him a hug. 'I'm going to miss your feet in my face.'

He laughs, and I shush him again.

Once inside my room, I strip off my grungy clothes and toss them into the laundry basket. I kick off Snow's shoes. I pull on a clean pair of pyjamas and get into bed. I have thirty minutes before my parents wake me up, and I'm going to use them.

✳ *Chapter Twenty-three* ✳

Maybe Stories Can Change

'Wake up, kids!' I hear. 'Time to get ready for school!' I open my eyes. I'm in my own bed.

Yes! I'm home! I'm home! I'm home! My watch and alarm clock say 7:00 A.M.

I can't help wondering, was it all a dream?

I run to my laundry basket. Snow's skirt and top are crumpled in my hamper. Her sandals are by my dresser. It happened! It REALLY happened!

I look up and spot my jewellery box on top of my dresser. Aw, there's Snow. Wait a sec, she's wearing something new. She's wearing...my lime-green pyjamas?!

161

Oh my goodness! We really did change her story!

I run into Jonah's room. His clock might be green, but he's fast asleep. I yank down his covers. 'It happened! It REALLY happened.'

'Tired,' he croaks. He opens one eye. 'Of course it happened. Why wouldn't it have?'

I run downstairs. Mum and Dad are in the kitchen. They're drinking coffee and rustling through the newspaper. I throw my arms around both of them. 'I love you guys!' I just hope they won't need their law books anytime soon. Or their computer chair.

My mum gives me a bowl of Coco Pops. Yay! How I missed the chocolatey yumminess! Yay! No more gross porridge!

Jonah comes running into the kitchen, yelling, 'Mum! Dad! Guess what? Abby and I swam with flying crocodiles!' He slides into his chair. 'Cool, huh?'

I put down my spoonful of Coco Pops and give him a look across the table. The mirror told us to keep it a secret. Not that I want to lie to my parents. But what if it puts them in danger? What if telling puts us *all* in danger? I'll have to give him a talking-to later.

'That sounds very exciting, Jonah,' my dad says, giving me a wink. He obviously doesn't believe him.

'Wow, Jonah,' Mum says. 'You're looking kind of

grimy.' She looks at me, too. 'So are you, honey. Didn't you take a bath last night?'

He nods his head. 'I did, but—'

'We were looking for something in the basement,' I say, jumping in. 'It was very dusty.'

'Did you find it?' Mum asks.

'Oh. Um. No,' I say. 'But we found other cool stuff instead.'

'It's very cluttered down there,' my dad says. 'We should give away some of the stuff.'

Cough, cough. 'It's, um, not that cluttered.' Not any more.

'Well,' Mum says. 'You'd both better take showers before school. Abby, you first. Hurry, 'kay?'

I down the rest of my cereal and then squeeze her tight. 'I'm so happy to be here,' I say.

My parents smile at each other. 'We're so glad to hear you say that,' Dad says. 'I know the move has been difficult for you – new things can be hard. Change can be hard.'

'I'll be okay,' I say. Change *is* hard. But it's not always bad. Take Snow, for instance. Her story is different now, but it's still good.

And take Smithville. It's still home, just a different home.

And freeze tag is still tag – just a different kind of tag.

163

Okay, fine. Freeze tag is still weird, but maybe it can be fun. I'll have to give it another try.

My dad squeezes my shoulder. 'What do you want for lunch, honey? Banana and peanut butter sandwich?'

Anything that isn't stew. 'Yes!' I say, nodding. 'But slice the banana.'

'Of course!'

I'm all for trying new things, but mushed banana and peanut butter glop are gross no matter which way you smush it.

I head back upstairs to take a quick shower and brush my very dirty teeth. I can't even remember the last time I used toothpaste. But on the way I hear a strange noise and I stop at the basement door.

'*Aaaaaaabby…*'

Was that my name? Should I go back downstairs and see what's happening? Is it Snow? Is she trying to tell us something? Is it Gabrielle? Or is it Maryrose? Who is Maryrose? Where is Maryrose? Is she in our mirror?

I'm about to open the door when I see my mum coming down the hallway. 'What are you doing?' she says. 'Go and get ready. I don't want you to be late.'

I let go of the door handle.

Tonight, I decide. Tonight I will find out why the mirror in our basement took us into a fairy tale.

Hissssssssss.
Definitely tonight.

Acknowledgements

Thank you thank you thank you to: Laura Dail; Tamar Rydzinski; AnnMarie Anderson; Abby McAden; Debra Dorfman; Becky Shapiro; Jennifer Black; Lizette Serrano; Becky Amsel; David Levithan; Elissa Ambrose; Tori, Carly, and Carol Adams; E. Lockhart; Lauren Myracle; Avery Carmichael; Courtney Sheinmel; Tricia Ready; Emily Bender; Aviva Mlynowski; Louisa Weiss; Larry Mlynowski; Targia Clarke; Anojja Shah; Lauren Kisilevsky; Susan Finkelberg-Sohmer; Judy Batalion; John and Vickie Swidler; Shari and Heather Endleman; Leslie Margolis; Meg Cabot; and BOB.

Extra love and kisses to Chloe, and my husband, Todd.

Read on for a sneak peek of Abby
and Jonah's next fairy tale adventure,

✳ *Chapter One* ✳

My Magic Mirror Might Be Broken

I have a magic mirror in my basement and I'm going to use it.

Jonah's hand hovers in front of the mirror. 'Ready?'

'Oh, yes.' I am definitely ready. I've been *trying* for three days. Four nights ago, Jonah and I accidentally got sucked through the mirror and landed in Snow White's fairy tale. Well, technically, we landed in the kingdom of Zamel. Rhymes with camel. That's where Snow White lives.

If I'd known we were going to Zamel, I never would have worn slippers and pyjamas. I would have worn jeans, a pretty jumper and trainers. But I didn't even know where we were until after we'd already messed up Snow's story.

But don't worry! Everything ended up fine. Different, but fine.

I did leave my slippers and pyjamas at Snow's, though. The slippers were pretty beaten-up anyway, but the pyjamas were my favourite pair. Snow borrowed them and lent me a skirt and top. Getting my pyjamas back isn't the only reason I want to visit Snow. I also want to know why Maryrose, the person who lives inside our magic mirror, sent me and Jonah there in the first place. There has to be a reason, right? And why did the magic mirror in Snow's bedroom tell us not to tell our parents about what happened?

Jonah and I decided to find out.

When we'd gone to Zamel, the mirror had sucked us inside at midnight, so the night after we got home, I set my alarm for 11:51 P.M. I put on jeans. A jumper. Trainers. I woke up my little brother, Jonah. He put on jeans. A jumper. Trainers. We crept down the two flights to the basement and closed the door behind us.

Jonah knocked. Then he knocked again. Then he knocked once more. Three times, just like the first time.

But it didn't work.

We stood there, waiting, but nothing happened.

No swirling. No hissing. No opening up its big mirror mouth and swallowing us whole.

The next night we tried again. We got up close to midnight. Put on jeans. Jumpers. Trainers. Crept down to the basement. Knocked and knocked again. Knocked a third time.

Nothing, nothing, nothing!

Tonight is Night Number Three. Everyone knows three's a charm. Especially when dealing with fairy tales.

So here I am. In the basement. Again.

Jonah's fist is up against the mirror. Again.

'Ready,' I say. I brace myself. Here we go. It's going to work. I know it is.

Jonah knocks.

Once.

Twice.

Three times.

No swirling, no hissing, no nothing.

I stomp my trainered foot. 'I don't get it!'

Jonah sighs in disappointment, and his skinny arm falls to his side. 'Do you think it's broken?'

I peer at the antique mirror. It looks the same as it did when we first went through it. It's twice the size of me. The glass part is clear and smooth. The frame is made of stone and decorated with carvings of small fairies with wings and wands. It's attached to the wall with heavy Frankenstein bolts. We just moved to Smithville – and into our new house – a few months ago, and the mirror came with the house. I used to think the mirror was creepy. I guess it's still kind of creepy.

But it's not *just* creepy. It's also fun. It's magic.

'It doesn't look broken,' I say, seeing my brother and myself in the reflection. Jonah's brown hair is short and kind of a mess, standing up in different directions. Mine is shoulder-length and wavy, but still neat. 'Let me try,' I add.

I knock once. Twice. Three times.

The room is still.

'Hello? Maryrose? Are you there?' I know I said Maryrose lives inside the mirror, but truthfully, I'm not sure. All I know is that Maryrose has something to do with the mirror. I think. I really don't know much. I sigh. 'Maybe we imagined the whole thing.'

'No way,' Jonah says. 'We were there. I know we were. We met Snow! We ate her stew sandwiches! Yum. I wish Mum and Dad would make them one night for dinner.'

I snort. First of all, Snow's stew sandwiches were gross. And second, the likelihood of Mum and Dad trying a new recipe these days is very slim. Like one in a bajillion. They haven't cooked in weeks. We've ordered pizza for the last two – no, make that three – nights in a row.

Don't get me wrong, I like pizza. What ten-year-old doesn't like pizza? What adult doesn't like pizza? Jonah LOVES pizza, even though he insists on dipping the crust in ketchup, which is totally gross. But three nights in a row is extreme. What happened to cooking? What happened to meat loaf? What happened to salad?

My parents used to cook all the time, before we moved to Smithville. They had time to cook then. Now they work all the time. They're lawyers and just started their own firm. I keep telling them I'm old enough to do the cooking, but they won't listen. Just because I nearly burned down our old house when I put my socks in the toaster ONE TIME. What can I say? I wanted toasty socks. They won't even let me near the washing machine, which makes no sense. Fine. I used too much detergent and turned the laundry room into a bubble bath, but also, only ONE TIME.

I yawn. 'Let's go back to bed.'

'But I want an adventure! Maybe the mirror can take us to other places, too. Like Africa! Or Mars! Or Buckingham Palace!'

'We've tried three times, Jonah. We can't do this every

night. We're growing kids. We need our sleep.'

He twists his bottom lip. 'Just one more try.'

I let him try one more time even though I KNOW it's not going to work. I am three years older than he is. I know these things. And I'm right. Of course I'm right. I'm always right. I march him up the stairs, back up to the top floor, and steer him toward his room.

He kicks off his trainers and plants his face on his bed.

Back in my room, as I change back into my second-favourite pair of pyjamas, I can't help but wonder if we really did imagine the whole thing.

But wait! My jewellery box is sitting on my dresser, and on the lid of my jewellery box are illustrations of fairy tale characters. Snow White is right between Cinderella and the Little Mermaid. Snow is definitely not wearing her puffy dress. She's wearing my lime-green pyjamas, which means it really *did* happen.

So why isn't the mirror working?

Read

WHAT Ever After

IF THE SHOE FITS

to find out what happens next!